I DO CHAOS

I DO CHAOS

A Model MD Novella

D. W. BROOKS

Cover design by 100covers.com

Publisher's Cataloging-in-Publication data

Names: Brooks, Dominique Walton, author.
Title: I do chaos : a model MD novella / D. W. Brooks.
Description: Houston, TX: Houston, TX, 2024.
Identifiers: LCCN: 2024902200 | ISBN: 979-8-9890807-3-1 (paperback) | 979-8-9890807-2-4 (Kindle)
Subjects: LCSH Physicians--Fiction. | Weddings--Fiction. | Marriage--Fiction. | African American women--Fiction. | Atlanta (Ga.)--Fiction. | Romance fiction. | Love stories. | BISAC FICTION / Romance / African American & Black | FICTION / Family Life / General FICTION / MedicalClassification: LCC PS3602 .R66 I46 2024 | DDC 813.6--dc23

Printed in Houston, TX USA.

Dedication

To my husband, who has offered so much amazing support during this journey and has dealt with my odd ideas and research plans.

Author Note

This story contains explicit content and topics that may be sensitive to some readers. For a more detailed topic list, please scan the QR code or visit https://authordwbrooks.com

I DO CHAOS

Prologue

On Friday morning, the loud crash of some unknown item in the distance startled Jamison Jones Scott out of a fitful sleep.

As she rolled over and slowly sat up, she struggled to open her eyes. She winced at the pain—her eyes were dry as hell, and her head didn't feel too great, either. Blinking furiously, she tried to assess her surroundings, hoping against hope that she was in her condo and her fiancé was sleeping next to her.

It was a faint hope that was quickly dashed.

She turned slightly to her right and saw an unfamiliar male lying on his stomach.

Not Eddie. *Definitely* not Eddie.

This guy was a dark-haired man—possibly Latino, Mediterranean, or just a white guy with a tan. The man turned his head toward her in his sleep so she could see his face. He looked *young*… at least younger than her 30 years. *Geez! Who the hell is this? Have I lost my mind? Was it possible to find a time machine to erase the last 24 hours?*

She blinked a couple more times to clear her vision and looked around the room. It reminded her of her room in college—sparsely furnished with a full-sized bed, a small dresser, and a few movie and concert posters taped to the wall. There were a couple of windows with no blinds or curtains, which showed Jamie that it was almost dawn. She looked back at her companion.

Seeing his face this time brought back flashes from the last night, with memories of multiple tequila shots, dirty talk, and flirting. Jamie muffled a groan with her left hand, the one with the three-carat antique engagement ring. She looked at it for a second and felt like the ring itself was accusing her of being a horrible fiancé.

And it wasn't wrong…

She turned the ring around backward to stop the accusatory glint from making her feel more guilty than she already was. Waves of remorse rolled off her, and her head throbbed as a byproduct of the many shots she downed last night. She shouldn't have gone to Buckhead last night.

On second thought, the original beer at the Buckhead Saloon with fellow residents from the hospital was not a bad idea. But it should have stopped there. The shots with a couple of fellow male patrons afterward were just a bad, no-good idea.

Just bad. She should have listened to her friend and left…

At least, the guy next to her was not a resident at the hospital. There would have been no way to keep this transgression from making it through the hospital grapevine, meaning that Eddie would hear about it.

One thing she did right… kind of…

Trying to get a handle on what happened last night was the next step. She didn't feel like she had sex last night. She looked down at herself and saw that her bra was still in place. Looking under the bedsheet, no underwear. *Damn.* Jamie lifted the sheet a little further to see the status of her bedmate. He had his underwear on. This didn't mean anything, but she was willing to grasp at any straw.

The best thing to do was to get out of here as soon as possible and try to forget that this had ever happened.

By now, the sun peeked over the horizon, and its light crept into the room, so it was no longer jet black. Jamie checked the floor on her side of the bed to find her missing clothing. Only her shoes were right next to the bed. She could only imagine the scenario that led to that event.

Scanning the other floor areas visible from her location, she spotted her skirt, shirt, and purse at the foot of the bed, but no panties. Jamie sighed. She wasn't getting up and walking around the room with no underwear, meaning she would have to take the sheet with her, which would likely wake her strange friend there.

Oh well…

Blushing as she tugged the sheet off the bed and wrapped herself in it, Jamie stood up and tiptoed to her discarded clothing. Kneeling with the sheet clutched to her chest made picking them up challenging, but she managed without falling on her face. Standing awkwardly, clothes in hand, she turned to see her bedmate sitting up, eying her with a smirk.

"Trying to sneak out on me, huh?"

His dark brown eyes twinkled at her as he seemed to find her discomfort amusing. Jamie wished she could be as relaxed about waking up with a stranger as he appeared to be. She averted her eyes. The young man didn't make any move to cover himself after she took the sheet off the bed. It could have been a very good morning indeed, judging from the bulge in his boxer briefs.

"Uh, no. I didn't want to wake you. I have to go." Jamie clutched the sheet tighter as she continued to look for her underwear.

Her companion leaned over to grab something from the floor on his side of the bed. As he sat up, he held up a little strip of fabric. "I think you're looking for these."

Jamie laughed uncomfortably and moved closer to grab her thong. "Thanks," she replied sheepishly, noticing that he had a muscular chest with an eagle tattoo on the right side.

Backing away, she dropped her clothes on the bed, turned her back to the young man, and slid her underwear under the sheet with some struggle. Grabbing her clothes again, she walked around to her side of the bed, sat down, and began maneuvering herself back into her shirt and skirt without removing the sheet.

Not an easy feat.

The man laughed. "The bathroom is next door, if that would make it easier for you. There's no one else here. They should all be gone to work." She could hear the faint Puerto Rican accent when he spoke.

"That's OK. I'm almost dressed." Jamie had her skirt on, but the shirt proved to be more of a challenge. She could feel his eyes on her back as she struggled to get her arms into her shirt under the sheet, which was weird because she spent several of her teenage years as a model, and here she was acting like a nervous schoolgirl.

"How about I go to the bathroom, and you can finish dressing," he suggested helpfully, hopping up and making a path through the scattered clothing on his side of the bed. Jamie seized that moment to drop the sheet so she could get the rest of her clothes on and slip on her shoes. After checking to ensure everything was in place and running her fingers through her hair, she neatly placed the sheet back on the bed. Grabbing her purse, she headed for the bedroom door and almost ran into her new friend—whose name she still did not remember—in the doorway.

They were approximately the same height (6'3"), as she had 4-inch heels plus her 5'11" frame. Up close, she could appreciate how handsome he was and why she went home with him. He had café au lait skin and a subtle 5 o'clock shadow. Full lips and straight nose. At least, she maintained her standards when picking a one-night stand.

Yeah, he was hot, but she was engaged. This reminded her she needed to know the details of last night, even if she didn't want to. Just to keep everyone safe. And with that, she was mortified again because she knew better than this.

He stepped to the side to let her pass. But seeing her cheeks redden again as she went by, he said, "My name is

Rey. We didn't have sex last night. I know you were wondering."

Jamie paused to look at him. "You're right; I was. But then, why was I half-naked?"

He chuckled. "Just because we didn't finish doesn't mean we didn't try. Just too much to drink. You fell asleep almost immediately after we got here. You did a mini striptease, including your panties. But you sat down and dozed off when you had trouble unhooking your bra." He rubbed his chin and gave a short laugh. "Doesn't say much about my game, does it?"

With no response from her, he reached out and gently caressed her jaw. "We can give it another try if you want," he added seductively.

A wave of relief washed over her. She didn't think they completed the deed based on how she felt down there, but that she had been this close did not speak well of her. "What a tempting offer. But I can't." She blushed again and tried to place a little distance between them. "I am sure your game was fine. It's me." Jamie smiled. "Take care. I really have to go." She turned back to walk to the front door.

"Oh yeah," Rey yelled after her. "I don't know where your car is. We took a taxi, Uber, or something here."

Ugh... more evidence of suspect decision-making. She just rode to an unknown location with an unknown person last night. Fortunately, she used Uber yesterday to get to the bar from the hospital. Therefore, her car should still be in the residents' parking lot. She would have to go back to the hospital, and hopefully, she could avoid anyone she knew well.

"Thanks for the heads up! Have a good one, and I'll see you around." Jamie escaped without revealing her name and, hopefully, maintained a smidgen of her dignity.

As Jamie walked out of the apartment into the early morning Atlanta light, she pulled up the Uber app on her phone. She didn't know what neighborhood she was currently in, which sent a chill down her spine. *Stupid, stupid....* Looking at the cross streets at the corner of the apartment building she had just vacated, she plugged that data into the app and waited for the rideshare to arrive. The streets were just getting busy with people heading off to work. Several of Rey's neighbors eyed her as they drove out of the apartment parking lot.

Was it that obvious? Jamie looked away and tried to look like she was unbothered. After 12 minutes, her ride arrived, and she slid guiltily into the car.

The driver, a Middle Eastern man, tried to entertain her with random facts and showbiz gossip until he got a good look at her face in the rearview mirror. He had been a cab driver before participating in rideshares and had taken part in many early morning rides. So, he knew that look. *The ride of shame...*

Jamie asked the Uber driver to take her to the hospital and replied once or twice to his questions. Once he stopped talking, she turned her attention to her story for Eddie. Telling him the straight truth was a no-go. She didn't understand why she was acting out right now and in ways that weren't her style. She had not been a cheater before, and infidelity was always her line in the sand. But now she was dancing right up to the line and sticking her foot over it. What was going on? With any luck, her fiancé had been called to the operating room last night. Was he even on call last night? More guilt washed over her. How the hell could she not know that?

This was just wrong. Should she even be engaged at this point? How did she get here?

1

T Minus 48 Hours
Morning Rounds

"**G**ood morning, everyone! Breakfast is here!" Pushing a cart filled with food, Dr. Jamison Jones Scott greeted her fellow residents and the office staff as she entered the dermatology clinic at 6:40 AM on that Thursday morning. Each resident was assigned a specific time slot to see patients in the clinic, no matter what rotation they were on, and Thursdays were hers. She sounded chipper than she felt despite the early hour.

During this early hour, Jamie had to present a short teaching lesson about blisters (how fun!). This was a new morning meeting because of one loudmouth medical student on a previous dermatology rotation. The student made an ill-advised comment about how cushy the dermatology rotation was, with no early rounds or late days. Of course, the attendings in the clinic took that appraisal to heart and decided that the residents would lead these short teaching sessions early in the morning on their specific clinic days.

Those early lectures—while inconvenient—did not make the dermatology rotation any more difficult for the students. The blowback was on the residents. While student attendance was mandatory while on a dermatology rotation, the residents had an additional presentation to plan. Other attendees for these sessions could include interns or residents from other departments who rotated through the dermatology clinic. Adding all the residents—dermatology and others—plus the nurses, nurse practitioners, and other assistants, the average attendance could be close to two dozen people. To ensure that people showed, Jamie always brought a substantial breakfast that included donuts, bagels, cream cheese, and juice.

Jamie had the food delivered to her condo first thing on those Thursday mornings. She worked out a schedule with a local bagel and donut shop for these early deliveries and paid a premium for the extra service. She usually would leave a bagel or two for her fiancé, and the rest went to the clinic. But this morning, she didn't leave him anything because the bagel count was short, and he didn't like to eat donuts for breakfast, although he was not an especially healthy eater. She hoped that one or two dermatology residents wouldn't show, so there would be enough food.

She should have taken the food issues as a bad omen for the day.

There were a few more than the customary attendees for today's talk. Some other hungry residents must have snuck in to eat the free food. Besides, for their presentations, the other residents were less imaginative with their breakfast selections: store-bought muffins or a few donuts. Not Jamie. The more mundane the topic, the better the breakfast. Her talks were always well attended, but this was above expectations. And on a day where she was a little short too!

Jamie placed all the food items on the table in the conference room. Someone already brought some plates, napkins, and cups from the supply kept in the small office kitchen. As soon as the boxes and bags left her hands, she got nudged out of the way so folks could have the first choice of breakfast items.

"Boston Cream! This is why I come to your lectures," Alana, one of the dermatology nurses, joked as she grabbed a napkin to pick up the aforementioned donut.

"And I thought it was because of all the wisdom I impart upon the masses," Jamie replied with a partial curtsey, which made the nurse laugh harder. She added, "Grab your food, everyone. I must run to the restroom, and then we can get started. Save me an iced cake donut, please."

Making her way out of the crowd around the food table, Jamie walked into the staff bathroom and checked her hair and makeup. She looked impeccable as always—her thick, flat-ironed brownish-black hair hung neatly down to her shoulder blades in a blunt cut. Her crisp, long, white jacket covered her white silk dolman shirt and black pencil skirt. Her almond-shaped brown eyes were accentuated with eyeliner and mascara, and her brown skin was smooth and even-toned. She didn't look very different from when she was a popular model in New York 15 years ago. She touched up her dark pink lip gloss. Nothing was out of place, but in her mind, she looked tired. Life was very hectic right now, and she wasn't enjoying it very much.

This presentation might be the highlight of her week.

Several life changes were all converging at once—and not in a good way. Finding a new job, planning a wedding, and transitioning from "student" to an actual working doctor, all simultaneously. All three were uncomfortable, but the first two were causing significant drama.

The new job: Jamie just applied for a rare open position at one of the leading dermatology clinics in the Atlanta area. One of the clinic's founders, Dr. Robin Henderson-Wu, had been the hospital's head of the dermatology department and played a role in selecting residents for the program (including Jamie). The practice was booming, and there were plans on the table to set up similar clinics in other locations, as well as to add additional specialties. Robin had big plans for Jamie.

For her part, Jamie went into the process, very excited about the possibilities. But throughout the interview process, she started to feel a little overwhelmed and less excited about the position. The reasons for her discomfort weren't totally clear to her, but the feelings were there. She continued with the discussions while trying to mask her uncertainty. The physicians at the clinic were making their decision any day now.

As for her wedding plans, it was a little over two months before her wedding in July. When she met Dr. Edward Boudreaux—better known as Eddie—over three years ago at a Grand Rounds medical meeting, Jamie thought he was cute and kind of earnest. Her best friend, Dr. Felice Hoffman, stood nearby and rolled her eyes as the pair low-key flirted with each other while standing by the bagels and cream cheese. They exchanged numbers and met for coffee a few times after that. Eddie's attitude toward her at the time was so platonic that Jamie thought he was angling to be a mentor figure in her life. Finally, he got the courage to ask her out on an official date two weeks later.

When Felice, who was also an internal medicine resident at the same hospital, found out about the future date, she shook her head but tried to hear her friend's point of view. Felice was a tall, blonde Jewish woman who Jamie met on the first day of med school. They bonded over the inanity of the first-day registration madness and had remained close ever since. They even ended up at the same hospital for their internship and residency training. Felice knew Jamie better than anyone.

Jamie excitedly ticked off all of Eddie's good qualities, of which he had many. He was very good on paper: a surgeon from an excellent family, tall enough (they were the same height), boyishly handsome, and her mother, Margaret Jameson Scott, would approve. Jamie omitted the issue of his more traditional expectations for his family life, which would require Jamie to curtail her career because she knew what her friend would say. Eddie had been very upfront about that during one of their coffee dates.

However, Felice had investigated on her own, as Jamie was her best friend, after all. It was common knowledge in the surgery department that Eddie wanted a wife that didn't work or only worked part time. Old-fashioned, sure, and it was cool that he wanted what he wanted. But Felice knew Jamie wouldn't want that… She tried to broach the subject gently.

"I hear you. He is good on paper. But you are ignoring the most important parts, Trey. You're not on the same page for the future," Felice replied with concern, using her nickname for her friend. Several people in med school—led by Felice—frequently joked with Jamie about her having three last names. Jamison was her mother's maiden name, Jones was her grandmother's maiden name, and Scott was her father's last name. So, she became Trey, short for Three Last Names.

"Don't worry. It'll be fine," Jamie said giddily. "It's just a date."

And so it began.

Eddie and Felice weren't so fine, though. Jamie tried to get the two of them to spend time together because it was crucial for the most important people in her life to at least get along. As Eddie thought Felice was "interesting" and Felice thought Eddie was all wrong for her friend, putting the two of them together became more and more difficult.

They didn't care for each other and refused to take part in Jamie's forced get-togethers.

Eddie's excuse for skipping the gatherings was, "She doesn't like me, Jamie. And she's a little wild. I can't believe you two are such good friends. Must be a case of opposites attract."

Jamie originally tried to explain the friendship: they went to med school together and had gone through a lot. Felice wasn't wild, but she knew how to have fun, which they had a lot of in school. Jamie was one of the first people that Felice came out to, which further cemented their friendship. Also, Felice was one of the few people who knew an important event from Jamie's history: that Jamie gave birth to a baby girl at 16 and put her up for adoption. Jamie got pregnant while she was a model in New York. Her mother found out and set up the adoption against Jamie's wishes. She was still dealing with it.

Eddie didn't know about that.

Fortunately, it didn't seem as if the fact that Felice was gay was the issue with Eddie—just a personality conflict. So, she hoped that, eventually, they would warm to each other after repeated exposure.

Felice expected things to not go well over the long run.

As the relationship progressed, Jamie admitted to herself that Eddie's desired plans for her future, including children, could be an issue. But she still wanted to wait to talk to Eddie about it. This was a discussion for a really serious relationship, right? Not that she ever got around to it, even after the engagement.

At that point, she and Felice agreed to disagree about the situation. They seemed to do that a lot when it came to Eddie. But the Eddie situation placed a wedge between them, and although Felice agreed to be at the wedding, the two friends hadn't spoken regularly in over a year.

Jamie snapped out of her reverie when another dermatology nurse, Kelis, poked her head into the bathroom and tapped on her watch.

"Are you OK in here? We need to get started, so you can finish in time for the clinic. And if you want that donut, you better get out here!" Kelis said. She frowned at Jamie standing in front of the mirror. "You know you look fabulous. Come on!"

Jamie laughed. With one last look, she turned, heading out to enthrall her captive audience with the ins and outs of blister management.

After the lecture, Jamie saw patients with various dermatological conditions during the morning clinic hours. The first-year residents working in the clinic during this rotation were rock stars, so they didn't ask her a lot of questions, making it an easy clinic.

While the front desk clerks checked out the last patients of the morning, Jamie gathered her things so she could go eat her lunch, some leftover chicken salad and crackers (made by her mother's housekeeper/cook). Jamie noticed, out of the corner of her eye, that there seemed to be a lot of commotion in the front of the clinic.

Looking up, Jamie spotted an important visitor entering the office. Dr. Robin Henderson-Wu, who rarely visited the clinic anymore, was in the building. Given her newfound indifference to the job she interviewed for, Jamie walked toward the conference room and away from the chatter. She planned to make a few phone calls as she ate and hopefully avoid her potential employer. To her surprise and chagrin, the woman stopped her before she could make her escape.

"Hi to the future Dr. Scott-Boudreaux. Oh, I'm sorry… are you planning to hyphenate your name?" Robin gave Jamie a quick hug, which was awkward. The Filipino Irish dermatologist was barely five feet tall and rarely wore heels at work, which was a significant contrast to Jamie, who had on heels. Despite Jamie's feelings during the interview process, Robin and Jamie became friends. They both loved talking dermatology and dreamed of practicing medicine in underserved areas one day. They also planned dinners and other outings with their respective mates to start after the job post was filled—no matter who got the job.

"Hi, Robin. How are you?" Jamie shifted her lunch to her other hand and backpack to the other shoulder to avoid an accident during the hug. "I considered keeping my name. But hearing you say it is making me reconsider!"

As she heard the words coming out of her mouth, Jamie felt like she was putting on a façade. *Like she had ever considered changing her name…* But this was her typical behavior since she got engaged—a big tendency to please and to go along just to get along. That needed to be unpacked. "I was just going into the conference room for lunch. What brings you over to the clinic today?" she continued.

"Looking for you, of course. I have something for you." Breathlessly, Robin reached into the black leather briefcase she was carrying and pulled out an envelope. "A contract for the position at the practice," Robin replied excitedly.

Jamie's eyes widened. *She got the job!* But oddly, she didn't feel excited. Jamie tried to plaster a dazzling smile on her face as her mind worked through the implications of this news.

Maybe she hoped she wouldn't get the job, so she could use that as an excuse to avoid all the things that were making her uncomfortable. If she worked at a different clinic—without all the family-friendly policies—she might be able to put off the childbearing portion of her life for a bit until she could get herself more prepared. She applied to other clinical positions as a backup plan. But now, that avenue of escape was closed.

Confused, Jamie began to feel claustrophobic, and the blood rushed from her head. Her heart was racing…*Is this what a panic attack looks like? The room was spinning.* Hyperventilating, she tried to force herself to calm down with minimal success.

Robin could see the sudden change in Jamie's demeanor and quickly called for help as she tried to guide her to a nearby chair before she collapsed on the floor. "Oh, dear. Maybe I shouldn't have just sprung it on you like that. Someone, get her some water!" Robin ordered.

Jamie sank onto the chair and leaned forward, head between her knees. She didn't expect to have this drastic of a reaction. But here she was, losing it at the mere mention of the job.

She needed to get herself together.

Robin asked someone to call Eddie. *Oh no*! Jamie tried to gather her wits to stop her, but nothing came out of her mouth. That was the last thing she needed.

Her fiancé was in surgery, but his scrub nurse placed the call on a speaker in the OR.

"Hello, who am I speaking to? Is Jamie alright? Maybe she needs to go to the ER to be checked out." Eddie inquired and suggested at the same time. There was an echo, and the beeping and hissing of the surgical instruments could be heard in the background. Eddie was worried but couldn't leave the colon resection surgery to come to check on her.

Alana came over and handed the phone to Jamie. Jamie slowly sat up in the chair and said, "I'm OK. I just… hadn't eaten… today. Just need to… take better care of myself. I'm feeling better. I just need to eat," she said to assure her worried man. Her voice started weakly, but strengthened as she went on. After taking a deep breath, she continued. "I'm so sorry to worry you. Get back to your patient—I'll talk to you later."

Eddie was reluctant to hang up, but his patient and the surgery required his attention. "I'll check on you as soon as I get out of this case," he told Jamie.

As she handed the phone back to the nurse, this situation reminded her why she should be very excited and happy about her upcoming nuptials. He sounded so worried about her. *Who wouldn't be glad to get hitched to a caring guy like that?* At the same time, she also found donuts and juice shoved in her face. She obliged, took a couple of bites of the iced-cake donut, and drank some of the juice offered. It made her feel better, so maybe her earlier reaction was because of low blood sugar.

Robin had been hovering around, concerned about her friend and potential colleague. When Jamie stood up to finish her trek to the conference room, Robin followed her. Once there, she made a beeline for a chair at the same conference table that held the food earlier in the morning.

"You gave me a scare," Robin disclosed, sitting at the large conference table across from Jamie. She slid the contract across the table. "I know this is a weird time to do this, but I want you to look at the terms later when you feel better."

Jamie gave her a small smile as she accepted the documents. "I'll look over them with Eddie and my attorney. Give me a few days. Is that OK?" she asked as she took another small sip of her juice.

"Of course. Especially after having you almost pass out in front of me." She looked at Jamie warily. "Is everything OK? You and Eddie doing alright?"

Jamie plastered another smile on her face. "We're fine. Just too much wedding planning. Our parents are trying to turn this into the event of the century!" Both women laughed and then paused for a moment of awkward silence.

Robin continued knowingly. "I know it can be a lot of pressure. Everyone expects a lot from you. Marrying into or being from a high-profile family can be nerve-wracking. When Alex and I got married, we went to the courthouse right before med school graduation. Our parents were not pleased, and to atone, we had to have big ceremonies in New York for my folks and in both San Francisco and Brazil for his large Japanese Brazilian family." Robin paused, then added, "That, my friend, is pressure."

"Yet you make it work. Marriage goals, right?" Jamie tucked a strand of hair behind her ear. "Can I ask a personal question?"

Robin nodded.

"How did you know it was real between you and Alex? Were you scared before you got married, before committing?" Jamie courteously probed.

Robin leaned back, lost in memories. "I knew in med school, our second year precisely, during a study session for pharmacology. We were just friends, edging toward more, but we didn't know that yet. I freaked out over a sample problem I missed, which led to me losing it about medical school and everything else. Full-on melt-down. He was so calm, and I was a mess." She laughed as she recounted the story. "Just like that, he calmed me down, reassured me, told me how capable I was. And it hit me. I needed—and wanted—that calm presence to counteract my crazy for the rest of my life. He felt the same way. And here we are, 23 years later."

Jamie looked down. She didn't think there was a specific moment like that in her relationship with Eddie. Robin looked at her quizzically.

"Oh. No one moment for you? You don't have to have a *moment*. That's our story. Everyone's story is different," she assured her.

"Sometimes, I wonder. I always thought I would be giddily planning my wedding, but it's not like that. Is it me? Or is there something wrong?" Jamie said absently. Suddenly, she snapped back to the present, where Robin was eying her with a look of concern. *What the hell—did I just say that out loud?* Jamie shook her head, gathered her belongings, including the employment contract, and rose from the table. "I'm sorry. Still feeling loopy from this morning! I shouldn't be droning on about my relationship with Eddie. We're fine. Two months and counting."

Robin jumped up, too. "Are you sure you're OK?" she asked.

"I'm fine," Jamie repeated quickly—*too quickly*. She needed to get out of there fast. *Too much over sharing!* "I need to review this contract and talk to Eddie. I'll get back to you ASAP. Thanks, Robin." Jamie slid out of the door of the conference room.

Robin watched her hurry away with concern.

I can't believe I told her all my business, Jamie thought as she walked out of the clinic. *And I didn't say thank you for the offer.* When she reached the atrium of the medical office building, she realized she didn't have a plan for her next destination, nor had she eaten her lunch, which had ended up back in her backpack in all the confusion. Jamie stopped to think about her options. She wanted to look at the contract and didn't have a clinic to attend in the afternoon. She had some time because she didn't have to go back into the office right away. The quietest place would be her car in the residents' parking lot.

Walking across the parking lot to her baby, her 1969 Black Camaro, she stood a moment and admired the lines of her antique muscle car. Sliding into the black leather driver's seat always had a calming effect on her. While the car was expensive to maintain, Jamie refused to get a more economical car. At least, not yet. Throwing her purse and backpack into her passenger's seat, she sat in the driver's seat and closed the door. The silence was comforting and allowed her to concentrate as she slid the contract out of the large manilla envelope.

Quickly reading through the terms, she couldn't find anything to complain about. The contract was generous. Six-figure per annum starting salary, six weeks of vacation, six weeks of sick leave, one week of call every six weeks, maternity leave, and the ability to adjust your schedule for part-time work after the birth of a child. Absolutely amazing. Yet, each time she read it, looking for some thread to pull to unravel this job offer, her heart started racing, and sweat trickled down her cheek.

Robin had gone out of her way to help her get into this position.

Perfect opportunity for her future life with Eddie, right?

To her credit, Jamie had once mentioned this discomfort to Eddie with little success. Of course, she didn't tell him she didn't want the job because she wasn't sure about having kids or altering her career.

Given the information he had, it was no wonder he brushed off her concerns. She knew talking to her mother about it was a lost cause, as her mother was already bragging about the job coup even before Jamie had been offered the position.

As she leaned back in her car seat to manage her emotions, her phone rang. It was her younger brother, Jonathan, who was an architect. Most notably, he was a bona fide ladies' man. He liked them in their very early 20s. Each relationship was on the fast track from inception to end—and generally ended very ugly. Jamie was very close to her brother and liked to remind him of his relationship follies regularly.

"Hi, Jon-Jon!" She answered.

"Jamie-Jay! How are you?" he answered. Although Jamie was 30 and Jon was 29, they often still used their childhood nicknames to address each other.

"Fine. What do you need? Is your girlfriend burning your clothes yet?" Jamie asked jokingly.

He snorted. "Nothing. Peyton and I are doing fine. Surprised?"

"After all of 10 days? Not surprised. Is she going to be your plus-one for the wedding? Or should we leave that place card blank so you can fill in the name yourself?" Jamie asked sarcastically. The likelihood that Jon would still be with Peyton, a very nice 22-year-old boutique manager, in two months was exceedingly small.

Jon hated when his sisters gave him a hard time about his dating life. He was young, not even 30 years old yet. Why should he settle down? He typically got away with the quick dating scenarios because he was good-looking, tall (6'3"), had a good job, and had a good sense of humor. Most women thought they would be the one woman to tie him down. He didn't want to argue that point on this call today, though.

"Whatever, sis. Who knows who I'll bring to your wedding? Anyway, this call is about the main event before the festivities. You know Eddie didn't want a roguish bachelor's party with debauchery and nakedness."

"Not a surprise," Jamie inserted.

"So, we're going to have a golf outing in wine country," Jon continued, ignoring her comment. "Do you think Eddie would enjoy a surprise stripper? A tasteful one, of course. The rest of the guys want to do something a little more like a bachelor party. Sipping wine all day isn't normal bachelor party shenanigans."

Typical all around, Jamie thought. Of course, the other guys would want to do something a bit more risqué during a bachelor weekend, even if it was in wine country. She told Eddie he could have whatever type of bachelor party he wanted as long as he kept his pants zipped and his body parts to himself. It didn't surprise her he went for the most conservative option available. That tendency was a little irritating.

"I think he would live through the stripper experience, but he wouldn't enjoy it very much."

Jon groaned. "I like Eddie, but he can be uptight. It's amazing that you two got together, eh? Opposites attract in a lot of ways. Don't worry; we'll try to liven him up during the weekend."

"Well, thank you, I guess," Jamie said, unsure if that was a good thing or not. She also paused at the comment about opposites attracting. It's not the first time Jon mentioned that. She didn't consider herself the wild partying type, but she had led a colorful life. She kept a lot of the details close to the vest, fearing self-incrimination. Eddie led a less dramatic existence. Would his normalcy plus her chaos make a long-term match? She thought so earlier in the relationship, but she had doubts now.

Tired of the tenor the conversation was taking, Jamie switched gears. "Oh, you need to call Mother. She wants you to bring her glass pans back to the house. And she's still annoyed that you didn't put the chicken into a travel container instead of taking the entire dish," she said.

The Scott family ate dinner together often. Although each of the three Scott children had their own residences—Jamie living with Eddie, Jon in a newly purchased home in Druid Hills, and sister, Jillian, and her husband, Richard, in Decatur—they spent a lot of time in the large mansion in Buckhead that the elder Scotts purchased when Jamie was

15. Jamie herself never lived there full time, as she was in New York working as a fashion model then. Jon and Jillian spent their teen years in that house. However, all three kids found themselves at the Scott compound at least once a week to visit and eat the delicious meals and desserts cooked by Olivia, their parents' housekeeper and cook.

"I had to take it all. Jillian wasn't sharing," Jon said indignantly.

"She's pregnant. You're supposed to let her go first!" She checked her watch. While she enjoyed talking to him, she had a lot of thinking to do. "Hey, Jon-Jon, I need to finish my lunch so I can get back to the clinic."

Lying, lying, lying…

"Cool, I have to get back to work, too. But I wanted to ask you something else." Pause. "Is everything OK with you? Jillian mentioned some resistance when she called you yesterday to ask about the seating chart for the reception dinner. Like you didn't want to participate."

Fu-- Jamie took a deep breath. She *didn't* care who sat where. She wouldn't *ever* care who sat where at any reception. In fact, she didn't want a sit-down dinner, so the tedium of a seating chart this size (400ish) was painful. Everyone wanted this super-formal event, but she wanted a lighter touch, like a cocktail party or mid-morning wedding with a brunch reception. Somehow, for her own wedding, she got voted down—even by her fiancé. Didn't leave a pleasant taste in her mouth.

It didn't feel like *her* wedding. They could still have a big, understated ceremony—something that would stand out if that's what they were trying to do—just earlier in the day. She also dreamed of having an "after wedding party" for actual friends and family. Make a day of it. But they all shot that down, too. So why was it shocking that she didn't care so much about the details? This wasn't her vision, and without Eddie's support, she didn't stand a chance, as both families wanted a big, elaborate function. And the parents were paying, so she thought letting them have their way wouldn't be so bad since she was getting the prize. But the situation pissed her off. Eddie particularly upset her because he laughed at her ideas. He walked it back later, but she hadn't forgotten.

"Honestly, why do they care what I think about this? I don't care about seating charts. I don't want to *have* seating charts. But no one cares what I want my wedding to be, so why are they asking about issues I don't care about? I don't want to know that Aunt Blah can't sit by Aunt Blah-Blah because 30 years ago, they fought…" Jamie paused.

Having a wedding wasn't even the most important thing... Given these conditions, she would consider a wedding at the courthouse—*if there was a wedding at all.* Eddie, on the other hand, was looking forward to the formality of the festivities… "Please, don't get me started on this again. I have to go back into the clinic, and I would rather not be furious and snapping at everyone," she added.

"Geez, I knew you weren't happy with how things were going, but *damn.* You hate the concept. You hate the guest list. It's almost like you hate the people involved. Why are you doing this again?"

Jamie leaned back in her seat. *Good question…*

"I wanted to marry Eddie?"

"Wanted?" Jon caught her slip of the tongue. But before he could follow up on her response, Jamie shut the conversation down.

"I have to go. The clinic is calling. Touch base later?" *Still lying…*

"Alright, but we'll talk. I have a date with Peyton tonight, so I won't be able to talk until tomorrow. Seriously, let's talk about this. I'm a little worried about you." He disconnected the call.

Jamie shook her head and looked at the contract in her hand again. Her brother's dates with Peyton were reaching critical mass. Sometime next week, the unraveling would begin—Jon's rapid uncoupling from a girlfriend of two to three weeks. The fallout varied, with some relationships ending with a whimper and others with a bang. Jamie couldn't worry about that now; she had her own messes to deal with.

She flipped through the contract again, still unable to find anything wrong with it. *Disappointing! It would be easier to turn it down if there were some unfavorable terms… wait, what?*

Putting the contract back in the envelope, she got out of her car, leaving her backpack behind. *I need to talk to Dad about this,* she thought. No need to ask Eddie right now. She needed to have an unbiased conversation with someone who wouldn't judge her for these weird feelings currently flooding her.

As she walked back into the clinic, Jamie remembered that she still hadn't eaten (lunch was still in the backpack), but she was so riled up that she probably couldn't have kept anything down if she wanted to. She quietly entered the back door of the clinic and made her way into the little office set up for the residents. Hopefully, no one in the office would look for her. Because she was on the consult service this afternoon, she was waiting for calls from inpatient wards in the hospital. It was one of the slower dermatology rotations because, although dermatologic emergencies existed, it seemed to be hit or miss with patients already admitted to the hospital. These types of emergencies showed up in the ER and the clinic. Consults was a rotation they were considering doing away with, but she, for one, was glad it still existed because it afforded her free time.

Her phone rang again; it was her other sibling, Jillian. Jillian was three years younger and originally planned to be a judge, with an eye to the Supreme Court, one day. But during her senior year in college, she met an older married attorney, fell in love, and got married in Hawaii as soon as he divorced. Now pregnant with her third child, the trajectory of her life changed. Most of the family didn't believe that the contentment she claimed with that new trajectory would continue, but who wanted to start any unnecessary drama?

"Hi, Jillian?" Jamie answered.

Jillian was already agitated.

Must have spoken to Jon. I will have to deal with him later.

"I just talked to Jon." Jamie nodded her head as she listened. Jon was often the peacemaker, but he often passed on information that might be better left unsaid. "Why are you being so difficult about things? I hoped that you, Mother, and I, could have some bonding time as we planned your wedding. But you act as if the process is a tedious chore. Why can't you look at the seating charts?" Jillian uttered from the other end of the phone.

Jamie spoke in a low, intense voice to not draw attention to herself in the office. "Because I didn't want there to be seating charts AT ALL. Everything I suggest gets shot down. Everyone else decides and wants me to smile and nod, even if it's not what I want." She was getting riled up again. "You, Mother, and Mrs. Boudreaux can look at them. I don't know most of the people anyway, and I don't care where they sit." She took a deep breath. "If you want to bond, let's talk about the open bar, which seems to be the only thing we agree on right now."

Jillian groaned. "I don't understand you! I would have killed to have Mother interested and happy about my wedding. You are just ungrateful!" Jillian was close to tears; Jamie could hear it in her voice.

Jamie took a moment before replying." Jillian, you know I supported you when you got married. But remember, you had the wedding and the reception *you* wanted." To smooth things over in the community since Jillian and Richard's relationship had been so scandalous, Margaret threw a big wedding reception six months after the elopement. It was an enormous success. "I am basically a participant in someone else's wedding fantasy. A wedding fashion show to introduce the wedding party? A long montage about Eddie and me, which includes almost all my old magazine covers and commercial ads? Wedding photos in each of the three outfit changes?" Jamie sighed. "It's a bit much."

Jillian couldn't be placated or swayed. "It's not *that* bad. You're getting the entire kitchen sink thrown at you and some luxurious honeymoon planned for you, and you still aren't happy. Mother all but disowned me when I got married."

Not true. But there was A LOT more to it, and Jillian knew that. Maybe the pregnancy hormones were making her more whiny than normal. "Look, Jillian, I love you. I don't have time for this pity party about your wedding history right now. I just want you to understand. You're asking me to do a ton of things that are not in my vision for my wedding and refusing to do any of the things I want. How happy should I be?"

"I'm just trying to help. I want you to be happy. Just hear what I have to say. And you'll be happy once you see everything! Also, we've planned the first bridal shower for 10 days from now. It's a housewares shower. There will be a lingerie shower and a travel shower, too. You don't have to be that involved. Just let us handle it. You'll see. It'll be beautiful, you and Eddie will be happy, and our kids will grow up together." Jillian was just rambling at this point. Jamie could tell that nothing she said penetrated Jillian's 'perfect wedding' brain. Some of it was probably a do-over for her sister because there was not much joy when she married. Just lots of whispers and secrecy—at least until their mother threw the wedding reception.

Jamie decided that resistance was futile at this point. To at least end the call on a pleasant note, she thanked Jillian, and they disconnected. This situation sounded like it was going to be excruciating. Maybe she could get Eddie to elope with her.

She called her father on both his cell phone and his office number, but he didn't answer. So, she left a message on each account. She then called Eddie, but he was back in surgery. She left a message and assured him she was fine and just needed to talk to him about something. Hopefully, they could make some decisions that they both felt good about.

After spending the afternoon sitting in the residents' office, Jamie had a quiet day with no consult calls. Only one resident stuck his head in to get her to look at a patient and offer her opinion. There was an attending physician already working in the clinic, but Arnold, the first-year resident, liked to ask Jamie, as the attending intimidated him. She tried to discourage that behavior, but the shy resident seemed to shrink in that doctor's presence. Jamie hoped that experience would help Arnold bolster his confidence. She wouldn't be around two months from now, so he needed to improve quickly.

Jamie checked her watch at 5 pm. Neither Eddie nor her father had called by then. *Unbelievable!* So, when her cell phone finally rang a few minutes later, she almost answered it without checking the display. But old habits, they say, die hard, so she took a quick peek—it was her mother. She was pretty sure Jillian had gotten in their mother's ear after the siblings' earlier conversation. For a couple of seconds, she considered not answering, but figured that would only cause more chaos. Margaret, her beloved mother, wanted things the way she wanted them, and if that required a little drama, so be it.

Margaret Jameson Scott was the matriarch of the Scott family. Originally from a wealthy African American family in Alabama, she attended college at Spelman University in Atlanta, where she met Gregory Scott, who was attending Morehouse University on a scholarship. Against her parents' wishes, she married him instead of the more established men they tried to pair her with. She and Gregory built a wonderful life with a thriving forensics and research lab and three successful children.

But while Margaret did not allow her parents to create a marriage match for her, she tried to pull similar strings with her daughters. Jillian avoided her intentions by marrying Richard. Margaret had fixed Jamie up a few times in the past, but by getting engaged to Eddie, Jamie exceeded Margaret's expectations.

The relationship with Eddie was a bit of a whirlwind at first. Even if they didn't agree on everything, Eddie was easy to talk to. They went to great restaurants and family gatherings and cooked together at home. Jamie got so swept up that she ignored the warning signs.

Yes, Eddie preferred she cut back on her workload or even stop working. Not what she wanted, but she went along. At first, quitting work sounded good on some days, right?

And he wanted a truckload of children. Jamie tried to skirt that discussion because she wasn't sure she wanted any kids right now or ever. She figured the lack of desire for children was associated with the daughter she gave up for adoption. But Eddie didn't know about either of those facts. And she thought her youthful mistake might tarnish her in Eddie's eyes.

Wasn't the fact she had mentioned none of this a problem, too?

She thought that with time, her feelings would change. She went to therapy again during the beginning of the relationship to work out some of her issues; however, she still didn't want to have babies at this point in her life. Actually, her therapist mentioned that the hang-up possibly was that she did not want to have kids *with* her fiancé, but Jamie poo-pooed that reasoning. She was sure it had to be about her earlier pregnancy and the entire adoption scenario. Really, she always considered herself someone who wanted to be a mom one day, right?

So, the glitter of the relationship and their status as the golden couple—surgeon and dermatologist ready to take over the world—kept Jamie silent. Her mother was over the moon when Eddie popped the question, giving her a 3+ carat diamond and sapphire ring from his grandmother.

Margaret and Jillian set about planning this grand gala to celebrate the union of two wealthy African American families in Atlanta. Jamie, at first, was in for this ride, but as the wedding got closer, she had to admit that Felice's characterization of a train wreck was eerily prescient.

Here goes. "Hello, Mother. How are you doing?" Jamie tried to assume a light tone.

"Don't 'hello' me. Dear, why are you harassing your sister, who is spending so much of her time planning the most important day in *your* life?"

Jamie rolled her eyes. "No one is harassing anyone. If anyone is being badgered, it's *me*. We have gone over this a few times. I now realize no one cares how I feel about it; thus, I don't want to go over it again. So, again I ask, how are you doing?" Jamie retorted, as she maintained an outward calm demeanor.

"Jamison Jones Scott." Jamie braced herself. Although her mother always called her by her complete first name, the full name salutation meant trouble. "Your ideas are *cute,* but inappropriate for an event of such magnitude. And your fiancé agrees with us. Why are you fighting so hard? Sometimes, I wonder how you snagged and kept a nice man like Edward. I mean, not your looks. You are absolutely gorgeous, if I say so myself. But your decision-making ability does not always match your intellect. You know I know this based on what happened in NY, but I have seen some improvements. But here you are making such a fuss about the wedding details. I just don't understand," Margaret stated.

Inhale, exhale. Inhale, exhale.

Anger and annoyance were bubbling just below the surface, but she wouldn't engage in a pissing match with her mother right now. "Since my ideas are so bad, why is anyone asking me anything? Just do what you want, and I guess I'll show up and smile for the cameras. I mean, why should I enjoy any of it? It's my wedding, but who cares? So, with respect, Mother, this is the last time I want to talk about this. I will be where you want me to be. Just don't insult me by asking my opinion and then telling me we can't do that over and over because you believe my ideas are stupid. It's exhausting."

"Jamison, why are you so angry? Both families decided on the big formal dinner…"

"Everyone but me. Continue," Jamie interjected.

Margaret blew right by that comment. "It fits with our standing in the community. A brunch wedding… I just don't see those often. They are for people trying to have a less expensive affair. Not appropriate for the Scott-Boudreaux wedding."

"It would have been different and stood out more. I wanted to have an after-wedding party for the families. But what does it matter? We are two months out now. This conversation is just rubbing salt into the wound. Can we stop?" Jamie pleaded for obvious reasons.

"Fine. Just stop attacking your sister. She is working hard for you."

"Again, not for me. For you." Jamie ran her hand through her hair. "All I know is this is supposed to be the best time of my life, and you folks are making me miserable. I'm not looking forward to this at all."

Margaret was alarmed at that statement. "You were a model, dear. I thought you would enjoy strutting around in wedding couture. Flaunt it, dear, while you still can."

"I didn't want my wedding day to be about my modeling days. I wanted it to be about me and Eddie, our love, and the love we share with our families. Not so sterile and orchestrated." Weary of this endless argument and feeling herself on the verge of tears, Jamie added, "I can't do this right now. I'll talk to you later. Have a good night, Mother."

Jamie hung up and buried her face in her hands. *I don't know if I'll last until the wedding.*

Her phone rang again. This time, it was Eddie—the one man she didn't want it to be. Not yet. She wanted to talk to her father first, but now that wasn't an option.

"Hey, babe," she said, working hard to modulate her voice.

"Hey. I got your messages. I just finished my last case, so I wanted to call you back. What's up?"

"They offered me the job."

Eddie gave a little cheer. "Perfect! Are there any limitations on how long you have to work before you move to part-time? Hopefully, we can plan to start our family sooner than later."

"Don't you want to be just us for a while? We can travel. We have both been in school and residency for years.

Working so hard… maybe we can just be a couple for a year or two and then try?"

"What? We discussed this. We both wanted a big family. You were on board. I mean, are you changing your mind?"

"There is just so much going on right now. Planning the wedding of everyone's dreams…"

"Aren't you excited yet? I know you weren't pleased about having a more formal event, but everything is being catered to you, so I figured you were happy now."

Jamie frowned. *Who the hell was she marrying?* She had been complaining at the condo for weeks—months even—was he not listening to her at all? "I hate the entire concept. You haven't heard what I have been saying?"

"I thought you were just venting. Just dealing with the planning. The process is stressful, according to everyone I know who got married. I figured you would work it out."

"Maybe there is a way to work it out." Jamie saw an opening and turned on her seductive voice. "How about you and I just fly somewhere next weekend and get married by ourselves? We can have a reception of whatever kind they want later. I want our wedding to be about *US*. Not showing we can throw a big party and flaunting everything. Something with more intimate elements. Could we do that?"

Eddie laughed. "Are you kidding? I am so excited about the ceremony. I can't wait to show the world my wife. And I am looking forward to the wedding fashion show. I never got to see you on the runway, so I think this is exciting."

Dismayed, Jamie replied, "But that's not wedding material. That has nothing to do with *us*. That's all about me and my past. And it's work. Why would I want to work during my own wedding? I got paid to do runway shows. Do you want to know my rates? You folks have lost your minds."

"I have an idea. What are you doing right now? I might be able to meet you in one of the residents' call rooms. I haven't seen you for a few days. I miss you." *Blowing right by the context of what she said.*

"What? I just called you crazy, and you jumped to sex?" This was starting to feel surreal.

Eddie was a little tired of the complaints about the wedding. It was just a ceremony. "Look, the parents want a big ceremony. They want to flex a bit. Why is that such a big deal?" He sounded a little exasperated, which Jamie detected.

She was exasperated, too. "They can flex anytime they want, but I thought this was our day."

"Baby, just relax. Let them have their fun. We have the rest of our lives together. Building that family that we have been dreaming of… It's just a day in a lifetime of days."

He sounded reasonable, but it was not just a day. And that building a family thing… they were far apart on a lot of things. She loved him, but was she willing to tie herself to a life and goal she didn't want or like? She didn't have long to figure this out.

"I'm sorry, I have to go. I'll try to give you a call later to see where you are," Jamie hurriedly got off the phone, tears welling up in her eyes, which meant her voice would be teary. She didn't want him to know she was crying.

Could this day get any worse? Escape looked like a great option right now. There were few people still in the clinic after hours, and no one was between her and the door. She could get away essentially unnoticed.

At least that went without a hitch...

As she left the building to go to her car for the second time today, Jamie ran into a group of three residents—two of whom she worked with during her internship. They were all dressed for a casual night out.

One of them, McKayla Matthews, MD, stopped her. Jamie tried to wipe her face quickly before her friend could see the tears.

"Hey, girl!" The young woman hugged Jamie in greeting. McKayla or Mac was a Caucasian woman who Jamie hung out with during their internship year. Mac entered a gastroenterology residency, so their paths diverged. But they were still friendly when they saw each other.

"I haven't seen you in a long time! You still look fabulous, but what would I expect? I hear you are getting married soon. Where is my invite?" Mac asked jokingly.

Jamie remembered why she liked to hang out with Mac in the past. The young woman tucked her vibrant red hair behind her ears as she laughed. Mac was a cute woman of average height and weight. Labels and a flashy appearance weren't important to her. Today, she had on a pair of skinny black low-rider jeans and a simple fitted black t-shirt. But her personality always seemed to attract guys, who Mac herself noted, "were out of her league." In the past, Mac had dated professional athletes, wealthy tech biz owners, and even a famous actor or two. It was a curse most women would love to have. "Seriously, how is everything?" she added.

Jamie smiled weakly, blinking furiously to hide the tears, and said, "Fine. Wild. Busy. It's so much sometimes that I'm not sure how I am."

"I totally understand. Wedding drama, I bet. My sister got married last year and told me not to do it *ever*. I'm resisting pressure from my boyfriend to make it official, because I don't need that right now." Mac nudged the young man standing next to her. "I don't know if you remember this guy—Frank Oden—but he gave in. He just proposed to his girlfriend. I told him to wait, but he didn't listen."

Frank blushed and laughed. "I remember you. Didn't we do an ICU rotation together?" He shrugged since the memories of those 24-hour shifts were hazy. "You're in dermatology, right?" he politely asked.

Jamie nodded and shook his hand. She remembered him as a quiet, friendly guy who she may have been on rotation with at some point. Internship year was a blur.

Mac then pointed to the other young man. "This is David Young, an allergy fellow. He's friends with my significant other." To him, Mac added, "This is Jamison Jones Scott, third year dermatology resident. We made it through internship hell together." She looked at Jamie out of the corner of her eye. "Are you busy? You look like you could use a drink. We're going to Buckhead Saloon for just *one* drink. After that, I have a prior engagement I can't miss. Join us!"

The men both joined the chorus to go out.

Jamie had a few moments before she needed to be home. Eddie would be at the hospital for a while, finishing up. Time for one drink, then she could return to the condo. A chance to postpone the hard conversation about the job and their relationship. "Why not? I have time for just one." Jamie said, holding up one finger and smiled. "Can I ride with one of you? If I remember correctly, parking can be impossible over there."

David chimed in. "Great memory! None of us want to deal with that, so we're taking an Uber." Just at that moment, the Uber driver pulled up.

Best offer she had all day.

Once inside the bar, the group could see some seats on the patio. It was a mild night, and it was early. The mostly millennial crowd hadn't arrived in force yet. It was still possible to hold a conversation outside and enjoy the evening air. David stayed inside to order everyone *one* beer—after all, they had patients to see tomorrow, right? Jamie, Mac, and Frank sat at a highboy table while waiting for David to return with their drinks.

Frank leaned forward and said, "I know we don't really know each other. But Mac's right. I just got engaged. Can you tell me what I am in for with all this wedding stuff?"

Jamie smiled at the chance to vent, with no one invalidating what she said. "I may not be the right person to ask. My 'wedding stuff'," she made air quotes with the words, "Is out of control at this point. I wanted a less formal event, but both families and my fiancé overruled me."

Frank scratched his head. "I thought it was the bride's day. Isn't that a rule? My girl bought a planner and several bridal magazines already. I just proposed last weekend."

Mac snorted. "This is only the beginning. Buckle up." Then she turned to Jamie. "So, I know you're marrying one of the hotshot surgeons—Boudreaux. You weren't dating him when you were an intern. I seem to remember you and Felice discussing some other resident."

At Jamie's look of astonishment, Mac laughed again. "You must not have listened to the intern gossip mill back then. We all knew something was going on between you and your resident, Austin something or other. Whatever his last name was. And that he thought you were cute, and there was some incident in a resident's room. But nothing really happened. I want the full story one day."

Frank grinned. "Even I knew about that!" Jamie feigned embarrassment, and the three of them laughed. The situation lifted her mood, and she was glad she had come out with them.

Mac continued. "You know there was so much curiosity about you! We heard about your backstory. You were this world-famous model! I remember seeing your magazine covers when I was younger. We watched everything you did!"

Jamie bowed her head and giggled. "I guess I didn't think about that very much. When I stopped modeling, I *stopped*. You know, I was on to my medical life. I hope I wasn't too much of a distraction."

"It was nice to have something else to think about besides the mind-numbing horror of being an intern," Mac replied. All three laughed again as David arrived with a bucket of Blue Moon beers with orange slices.

As they all dug into their beers, a young blond woman in a short black dress tapped Frank on the shoulder and whispered into his ear. He then tapped David, who jumped up and hugged the new woman. Frank leaned over and said to his female companions, "They went out a few years ago. She's the one that got away for David. Could you excuse us for a moment? There are a couple of friends two tables over—we'll be back."

Once they left, Mac sat back, ready to dish. "Now, tell me. It's just us. What's going on with your wedding? I have seen Dr. Boudreaux. You did well!" She nudged Jamie with a wink. "Have you lost control of your wedding? Will they not allow you to be a bridezilla?"

Any other person asking these questions would have pissed Jamie off. But this was an opportunity to talk to someone with no judgment, which was something she hadn't been able to do very often over the past few months.

"Well. That's difficult to answer." Jamie took another sip to build her nerve. "I shouldn't be telling you this, but you're the first person I have talked to outside of my family about anything of significance since I got engaged. It's my fault because I don't have many girlfriends."

"What happened to your friend, Felice? You two were inseparable. You aren't talking anymore?"

"She's in the wedding, which surprises me. She doesn't think I should marry Eddie. We aren't right for each other, according to her. I ignored her at first—which hurt our friendship—but now I wonder if she was right." A few tears rolled down her cheeks. "Sorry, I don't know where that came from. Must be the beer."

Mac sat there quietly as Jamie tried to compose herself. The crowd picked up slightly, but it was still not super noisy. They had only been there for a little over 30 minutes. A lot had happened in that time.

"This is so embarrassing! I bet you wish you hadn't stopped me today!" Jamie joked.

"You're fine." Mac took another sip. "Actually, I am glad you're talking. You looked tightly wound when you walked out of the building. Way more than you were as an intern. Everyone changes, but you seem different."

"How do you mean?" Jamie asked, a bit confused.

"I don't know. You were so confident back then. We all wanted to know about you. You were smart and glamorous. A star in our midst."

"Not so shiny right now, huh?" Jamie smiled. "Honestly, it's the bluntest anyone has been with me since Felice. There is something wrong. I'm marrying a wonderful guy who wants a different future than I do. I know this, but I'm mindlessly following along. And I'm not sure why." She paused and looked around. "I need a shot if I'm going to keep spilling my guts."

Mac snickered. "I'm sticking to one beer—clinic in the morning. Anyway, I have to meet my sister after I leave here. Then home to my boyfriend, who remains just a boyfriend."

"Why don't you want to make it official? You just lit up when you mentioned him."

"I love him. I really do. But I'm not ready for what marriage to him would entail. He is part of a wealthy family—I suspect you are having some of the same issues with the Boudreaux family and your own!" Mac laughed for a moment and took another sip. "As for me, I'd have to alter my lifestyle to marry him. It's nice not having to answer for my time. Or go to fancy gatherings. Or discuss when we're having babies. I'm still young. We have fun and travel when we can. We don't want kids yet, so why do we have to get married now? It works for us. Does Eddie want kids?"

"He wants them *immediately*."

"And you don't?"

"I don't. I think I thought I did, or I would by now. But I don't. I'm not ready to have another one…"

Mac almost dropped her drink. "I was planning to leave, but this is getting interesting. *You had a baby*? When?"

"I was 16. It's why I left modeling full time."

"Where is the baby? Sorry if that's too personal." Mac asked.

Jamie was relieved to talk about the situation. "My mom arranged for her adoption. I was a mess. The baby's father had just ODed. I had an eating disorder and was afraid to tell my parents. Giving the baby up was probably the right thing, but I haven't made my peace yet. That's a whole other story."

"That's a problem. Does Eddie know all of this?"

"Only if my mother told him. It feels good to tell someone. My siblings don't know either."

Mac leaned forward. "Here is my unsolicited advice: you can't marry Eddie without telling him everything. It's not fair to either of you." She checked her watch. "Damn, I want to talk more, but I have to meet my sister. If I blow her off again, she'll never let me live it down."

"I understand. Just talking helped with some clarity," Jamie noted.

Mac finished the last gulp of beer and stood up. The saloon was crowded now, and Mac worked to maintain her footing as roving bar patrons jostled her as they looked for a seat. "If you want to talk again, you know how to find me." She put her hand on Jamie's shoulder. "And you know this stays with me. Are you leaving? Can we Uber over together to the residents' parking lot?"

"No, I think I need another drink before I go home."

"I don't want to leave you here alone." Mac frowned. "I would feel better if you let me drop you back at the hospital or even at home. You don't need to be driving."

"I'm OK," Jamie said and held up her right hand. "I promise not to drive. Just one more shot and then home."

Mac shrugged and agreed as she looked into her cross-body bag for money to give David for her beer on the way out. "O-o-o-k. It has been good catching up with you. We need to do this again sometime." She smiled at her. "You need girlfriends."

Jamie stood up, and Mac hugged her. Mac kissed her on the cheek and patted her on the shoulder before walking over to where Frank and David were still carrying on their conversation.

Jamie watched Mac exchange a few words with the young men and then head out of the bar. She was certain that the topic of conversation was her, and sure enough, both men looked back at Jamie and motioned for her to come over. She held up one finger for a minute and took that time to finish her beer. While sitting at the highboy table, Jamie considered what she and Mac had discussed. Mac wasn't wrong. She really couldn't get married without Eddie knowing everything. And the likelihood of there being a wedding if she told him everything tonight—the adoption, not wanting kids, wanting to work—was pretty small.

She truly screwed this up…all of it.

After a couple of minutes, she could see a small group of patrons hovering around, hoping she was vacating the table. As she stood, she made a sweeping gesture to the waiting customers, who gratefully dove at the table. Jamie spent a moment chatting with David, Frank, and their friends, but quickly excused herself with the explanation that she was getting one more drink and leaving.

As she walked to the bar, Jamie decided to take a step toward fixing some of what she broke. She pulled out her phone and typed up a concise email to Dr. Henderson-Wu, respectfully declining the job offer. While composing the mail, it was like she was in a different world, and all the surrounding clamor just fell away. She hadn't figured out what came after she sent this email, but she knew she needed to make some changes and grab control of her life again. This was the first domino…

Send.

She exhaled. This probably put her wedding plans on pause, if not on cancel. The weight of that email almost knocked the wind out of her. *What had she just done?*

Gradually, all the surrounding noise crept back in as someone walking by jostled her out of her reverie. She made her way to the bar and ordered a Woo Woo shot with peach liquor, vodka, and cranberry juice. This would provide a nice kick, but keep her from falling flat on her ass. She had to deal with Eddie when she got home.

A man to her right said to the bartender, "Add that to my tab."

Jamie looked over at him and grinned. "Thank you, but I have a fiancé," she leaned closer to his ear so he could hear her. He was really good-looking.

"Great, and congratulations. It's just a drink." He already had a bourbon neat in his hand. "It means nothing. But if you want another one, let me know." He smiled back—a crooked, sexy smile—and drained his glass.

She smiled back. What could one drink hurt?

Best laid plans…

2
T minus 24 hours

After being dropped off in front of the hospital by the Uber driver around 7:15 AM, Jamie was relieved to reach her car, which sat in the back of the resident's parking lot. She checked her watch and guessed she would have enough time to go to the condo she shared with Eddie, shower, and return to the clinic by 9:30 am. Fortunately, today would probably be another light day on the consult rotation. After what she did last night, she wouldn't be surprised if the attendings locked her out of the clinic. Fortunately, she could consult from anywhere because the clinic didn't have to see her at all! She would go in if anyone called.

As she pulled up in front of their condo in Midtown, she tried to plan how she could avoid going into the clinic again. It would be difficult to avoid Henderson-Wu for the six weeks left in her residency—although it could be done. She could do a rotation somewhere else, as she had already completed all her requirements. While she still believed she did the right thing, she questioned her methods—another instance of leaping before she looked…just more chaos.

Scanning the condo garage as she scanned the lot while she was at the hospital, Jamie didn't see Eddie's truck. She never understood how he planned to have a gaggle of children when he refused to give up the regular cab pickup. But it made his vehicle easier to spot.

He hadn't parked in one of the two designated spots for their penthouse unit. *Whew…*

Grabbing her purse and backpack, she scooted out of her car and made her way to the elevator. Their unit was the penthouse on the 31st floor. A bit extravagant for two residents, right? At the news of the engagement, both sets of parents volunteered to chip in to help purchase their first home together. Jamie managed to stave off her parents, but Eddie was less successful. So, they moved into a penthouse.

The logic behind getting such a nice condo was sound. Neither of them had time to manage all the ins and outs of a stand-alone house, and buying a condo would leave options for rentals or other family members taking over the space once Jamie and Eddie purchased a house. This planning was one reason the Boudreaux family had done so well financially.

Jamie took a deep breath as she entered their home. When they first moved in, she managed the condo decorations and gave it a mid-century contemporary style: the tufted back fabric sofa with a tapered leg ottoman and decorative accent tables. Hardwood floors throughout with lush accent rugs. A thoroughly modern kitchen and a framed photo of Jamie's first fashion magazine cover. Eddie found a clean version and had it framed for their first anniversary. Dropping her purse on the couch, Jamie walked over to the photo and examined it as she had many times before. She had been 15 at the time the photographer took this shot and at the height of her modeling powers. This was right before she met Zach, the drug-addicted photographer she thought was her one true love. Before the baby…

Jamie felt herself slipping into a pity party and gave herself a mental head slap. Preoccupied, she walked into the master bedroom, where Eddie was sitting in an armchair in the corner. Waiting for her…

Jamie gasped.

He looked tired—more tired than she had ever seen him. Even after a long day of surgery, he didn't typically look this weary.

"Eddie," she said as she dropped her backpack on the king-sized bed. "I thought you were at the hospital." Given the look on his face, she decided not to give him her customary kiss. Besides, she hadn't showered yet and didn't feel right, given she had just gotten out of another man's bed.

"I was at the hospital this morning. But I was here last night." He rubbed his forehead in frustration. "You didn't come home last night. Where were you? I was worried."

Damn, damn, damn. She slid her shoes off and headed toward the *en suite* bathroom. "I had a drink with Mac—remember her? Then I went back to the hospital and crashed in an on-call room for a few hours," she yelled over her shoulder. Jamie looked at herself in the mirror. She could see the shame and guilt in her almond-shaped eyes. Her brown skin looked ashen, like she had been out in a bar with smoke and booze for too long. She took a deep breath and stuck her head back out the bathroom door.

"I feel gross. I have to jump in the shower." Before she could fully retreat into the bathroom, Eddie asked, "When were you going to tell me you turned down the job with Henderson-Wu and Associates?"

Jamie hadn't fully prepared herself for that question, as she thought she had more time. "It just wasn't the right position," she said lightly, knowing that her statement sounded ridiculous, and that Eddie knew it. "Can we discuss this after I get out of the shower? Or do you have to get back to the hospital?"

Eddie stood up. His handsome, boyish face looked stormy. "Oh. No. I got someone to cover for me. We have time." He cocked his head. "Go, get cleaned up. I have questions, but they'll wait." He walked out and headed to the kitchen to get himself a shot of bourbon. Eddie was not much of a day drinker at all, but the past few weeks with the woman he loved was driving him to drink. He noticed that as the wedding date neared, Jamie had become more and more unpredictable, which was so unlike her.

When Eddie met Jamie at Grand Rounds over three years ago, it wasn't the first time he noticed her. A tall, gorgeous African American resident garnered the attention of all male residents and attendings (and some females)—married or single. Her reputation as a former model in New York proceeded her, and she didn't do much to hide it. Even after a night on-call (in either dermatology or internal medicine), she always looked put-together with lip gloss, mascara, and eyeliner, hair arranged just so. She was not quite model thin anymore, but her legs were still miles long and perfect as far as anyone could see.

She was hot.

It took a week or two for him to build up his courage to talk to her. He was handsome in a boyish way, and it was difficult for him to grow a mustache, even now. She was probably used to glamorous dudes. He was a nice guy and figured he had no chance with her. His boys backed him up in that assessment.

At the refreshment table for a Grand Rounds meeting, Eddie finally got the nerve to speak to her over the bagels and muffins. Some lame line, but to his surprise, she seemed receptive. They met for coffee once or twice casually, and then he asked her out to dinner at the legendary Paschal's restaurant. He impressed Jamie with his choice of establishment, and the date went smashingly. And they were off to the races.

The beginning of a dream…

The first time they made love, Eddie knew this was the woman he wanted to spend his life with. He was a surgeon, so it wasn't like he was struggling in the female department. He also came from a wealthy family, so he'd spent time with sophisticated, gorgeous women. But there was something different about her for him. He put her on a pedestal, which is probably why he didn't yell at her when she came into the bedroom after staying out all night. He brushed any questionable behavior under the rug because he thought the sun rose and set on her. She knew it and used it to her advantage.

But not today…

After Eddie vacated the room, Jamie immediately tossed on a shower cap and jumped in the shower, hoping to stretch out the time before this fateful conversation. She stood in the stall, letting the warm water attempt to wash away her guilt and confusion. Maybe the steam could help clear her head.

What did she want to say to Eddie? She turned the dermatology position down. Which felt right in the moment, but how could she explain it? The job was tailor made for what her life was supposed to be with banker's hours three days a week and one-half day, call every couple of months. And the key was the ability to tailor her schedule in the future as they had children. Honestly, this was the best scenario she could have imagined, which was why the position was so sought after.

But when she received the offer letter, Jamie panicked. In the office. In front of her potential boss. That can't be the appropriate reaction to getting your dream job. Did she make the right decision?

As she scrubbed her body to get rid of all traces of Rey from her body and mind, she asked herself that question again. Did she not want what she currently had: the perfect life with the respectable cute surgeon husband? The merging of two wealthy Black families in Atlanta? Two doctors…the stories wrote themselves. Both families were over the moon, but this was true, especially for Jamie's mother. Jamie knew status was important to Margaret Jameson Scott, and this marriage had it in spades. You might think that her mother was the one getting married.

As her mother's oldest surviving child, she knew she was the holder of many of Margaret's greatest aspirations. She was the golden child, as Jaime's younger siblings, Jillian and Jonathan, were well aware. Jamie started out well, but she got pregnant, shattering all her mother's expectations. Jamie spent the intervening years trying to make up for that.

She recognized this, but felt powerless or unwilling to change her life trajectory until now. Jamie knew she had been making choices that would please her mother, often more than herself, to make amends for her error. It was a problem.

But Eddie…was she with him just for her mother's happiness? She loved him, loved having sex with him, and he loved her ass through thick and thin. That was hard to give up. But she didn't want the life he wanted as a stay-at-home mom with kids. Eddie wasn't an adventurous traveler, and there were a lot of places that Jamie wanted to visit. They didn't want the same things, but Jamie had been going along to meet expectations. One day she was going to wake up bored, just as her friend Felice said.

This couldn't stand. She turned off the shower and wrapped herself in a big fluffy black towel as she tried to clarify her thoughts and what she wanted to say.

When Eddie proposed, part of her was over the moon, but a small voice kept whispering, "No!" It was almost like an out-of-body experience. She could see herself saying yes and accepting the ring like it was someone else's life. It wasn't an awful life, just not hers.

As the wedding got closer, she became more irritable while Eddie got more excited. He asked about getting rid of her birth control pills and trying to start a family within the first year. The cold sweat appeared again, and she played it off.

Just needed some time, huh?

She started going out more with friends and flirting with other dudes. Last night was the worse example of that. She was trying to get out of her life without standing up and taking command of her future.

Jamie sat on the bed and applied lotion all over her body. She knew that the situation they were in was mainly her fault. She needed to say what she wanted. Maybe with more therapy, she could handle her issues. But even with outside help, she couldn't resolve her problems in two months. She had to make some decisions, and today was just as good a day as any.

She put on another sleek black pencil skirt (her favorite), a sleeveless yellow scoop neck tank, and a pair of 4-inch black high-heeled pumps. She combed and brushed her hair. Once she and Eddie started dating, she allowed her hair to grow and kept it straightened. She sported a short curly asymmetrical bob during medical school and threatened to shave the sides at one point. But Eddie preferred it longer.

She looked at herself in the 3-way mirror in the walk-in closet. She looked good—better than she felt. This outfit was like a suit of armor. She was prepared for whatever came next.

Eddie was sitting at the breakfast bar in the kitchen as she came downstairs. An empty shot glass sat in front of him. Jamie knew that meant he was gearing up for a tough conversation. She pointed at it and gave him a little smile.

"Is it going to be that bad?" she asked as she went to the fridge and looked in. She needed to have something to drink—something to hold so she could keep her hands busy.

"I actually don't know how bad it's going to be," Eddie replied. "I know we need to talk about what's going on, whatever it is." He put his elbow on the bar and placed his chin in his hand. "What's happening here? You seem off."

Jamie selected a bottle of iced tea from the fridge. Taking a sip, she plunged ahead. "I'm sorry I didn't talk to you about the job. I turned it down because I want a position that'll be more challenging."

Eddie frowned. "What? I thought the plan was to find a job that would allow you to stay home with our kids for a while and then return part-time. I thought we were aligned on that goal…"

Now or never… "I have said I wasn't sure if that was how I wanted to do things." Jamie cut in.

"You mentioned that, but we talked about it…"

"You talked; I listened. And *you* decided. I don't want to stay at home. An extended maternity leave, maybe… I spent a lot of time in school. I want to practice, to work."

Eddie sighed. "It didn't seem to be that big of a deal to you when we first started talking about this."

"That's my fault," Jamie said. "I thought it wasn't, but it became a bigger deal the more I considered it."

Eddie could see a bit of his dream life that he envisioned crumbling as they talked. "And you didn't mention it every time I mentioned staying at home. You just let me talk about it without chiming in, *'I don't want that'*?" He squinted at her face because she had gone pale. "Is there something else you don't want that I should know about?"

It was already well past time to let her feelings be known. "I don't want a big family. Unless I can have twins or triplets." She tried to lighten the mood, but she could see that wasn't happening.

"How many kids *do* you want?"

"I don't know—maybe one or two. In a few years…"

"*Maybe* one or two? Aren't you the woman who sat and named our future kids with me?" Eddie got up from the barstool and started to pace. "I don't like where this is going. I don't feel like I know you right now. Two of the biggest things we discussed and planned for, you don't even want." He shook his head. "And it's not like you tried to talk to me about it, and I shot you down. You went along with the planning!" His voice went up a little by the end of his comment.

"I'm sorry." She tried to take another sip of her tea, but her hands were shaking. "But we need to talk about it now before we end up in a mess."

"Ok." Eddie sat back down on the bar stool and took a deep breath. "Do you want to have a baby within the first—let's say—two years of marriage?"

She bit her lip. "No. Maybe start trying during the third year?" This answer still sounded fake in her head, but old habits die hard.

A little more of his vision crumbled. "I'm in my early 30s, and you are 30. If we wanted to have several kids, we would need to start sooner rather than later. That was always my thought. I have several brothers and a sister. I loved growing up in a loud house, and I wanted to give that to my kids." He eyed her. "Do you really *want* kids?"

"Some days, I do. Others not so much." She almost told him about her teen pregnancy, but something held her back. She wasn't sure she wanted to pull the plug on this entire relationship yet and telling him that right now would probably do just that. "With the wedding coming up, it's hard for me to think about kids. Right now, I feel a little overwhelmed." She came around the bar and sat down. "I would be the one carrying them and pushing them out and nursing and changing. I worry it will take over my life."

"So, I'm confused. I am now marrying a full-time working woman who may have one kid and then hire a nanny?" Eddie retorted.

"That's not exactly what I said. But would that be the worst thing?" She could feel things slipping away, and her eyes welled up.

Eddie came over and stood directly in front of her. *God, she was beautiful.* Maybe that blinded him to some differences he seemed to have missed. "Do you love me?" he asked.

"Y-y-yes," she stammered. Was that not a ringing endorsement of her feelings, or was it because she was crying now? He hated to see her cry.

"That didn't sound all that convincing. Do you want to marry me?" He wiped away a tear from her cheek with his thumb.

This was the question she didn't have an actual answer for—the one she hoped he wouldn't ask. She ducked her head and mumbled, "I don't know."

That actually shocked him. With all the revelations, he thought they had some intense work ahead of them. Now, she wasn't sure about the marriage itself. How could he have been so wrong? His vision disintegrated right then. He went to sit on the couch with his head in his hands.

She followed him and sat next to him. "Hey, I'm confused. We are changing the parameters of our relationship on-the-fly right now. I can't believe you are sure about everything we've just said."

He looked at her and said quietly, "I would go to the ends of the Earth for you."

Her heart broke. She couldn't say it back—not that he expected her to. The way he looked at her, she was embarrassed to say, was a turn-on. Could they fix this? Would sex right now help? She leaned in, kissed him softly, and cupped his face with her hands, with their foreheads touching. She felt a rush of sadness for the impending loss—she had once imagined a little boy that looked just like his daddy.

"I love you," she whispered.

"I love you, too." He cradled her hand and kissed the pulse point at the base of her wrist.

Definitely not a fair fight.

Without an actual idea of what this might mean, they undressed and made love on the couch. It was slow and tender, and when Jamie looked back on it, it was like a goodbye. Afterward, they lay intertwined on the couch for about 10 minutes, with Eddie taking their lovemaking as a reason to hope. Jamie snuggled in silence, listening to his breathing.

She knew then she couldn't marry him.

It wouldn't be fair, and she needed to get her own hopes and dreams together before she foisted them off on someone else. The man she married, she would need to be able to tell about the daughter she put up for adoption and that entire NY situation. She had been too afraid to tell Eddie because she thought he would look at her differently. She had been too weak and would never know what his reaction would have been. Sadly, it was too late now.

Eddie's phone rang. One of his patients was having a minor issue, and the resident covering his service wanted him to come into the hospital for a second opinion. He jumped in the shower as she followed him to the bathroom. She sat on the closed toilet seat as they made small talk and asked him about his patient. As he got dressed and headed out the door, he looked at her and asked, "Can we have a serious talk about this tonight? I want to fix this."

Tears in her eyes, she repeated, "Tonight." And kissed him on the lips again.

As soon as he left the condo, Jamie grabbed her phone and googled "same day movers".

For a premium, you can find movers to come pack and move your stuff out immediately on the same day.

Jamie figured that service was available. The first company she contacted seemed eager for the job, especially since she wasn't taking any furniture. Jamie just wanted to get her clothes, a few photos/paintings, and knickknacks out. A pretty simple job. That movers who moved people out of their homes on the fly exist might suggest that people in failed relationships wanted to escape shared homes with quickness. She could relate. She was on a timeline, too.

After scheduling the arrival time—one hour—she headed back into the bedroom. As she placed her belongings into suitcases, she had moments of self-doubt. Why was she leaving like this? Eddie had done nothing wrong, and they *could* talk.

Her brain squashed that train of thought immediately. There was no way she wouldn't end up married in two months if she stayed. She knew herself and how weak her resolve was around this situation and this man. She needed to get out now and fix herself first. Maybe she and Eddie could revisit their relationship after some time and space. That sounded good, but she knew it wasn't likely.

3

T Minus 12 Hours

<hr>

Margaret sat at her kitchen table, flipping through the household mail. Bills in one pile, personal mail in another, and junk mail straight into the trash can. Most of the bills were on autopay, but she reviewed all statements monthly.

Boring task but necessary. She was a little more energized today because, in a few minutes, there would be no one else at the house for the afternoon.

She could get a little peace.

Her husband was planning to stay late at the lab to work on a research project, and her housekeeper, Olivia, who had been with the family for over 10 years, was tidying up and prepping for a long weekend of visiting her children. The housekeeper/cook prepared several dishes that could be popped into the oven, which also worked well as leftovers. Bacon, spinach, and cheese quiche topped the list, and with no children or grandchildren expected to visit this weekend, the quiche should last for over three meals if desired. While Margaret could cook for herself and her spouse, Olivia liked to give her employer options when she was away from their home or out of town.

Margaret's children seemed to all have reached reasonable places in their lives and weren't likely to appear on the doorstep to crash in their childhood rooms. It surprised people who knew Margaret that she had an open-door policy toward her children. Basically, they could come back and stay at any point. She had room in the home. *Why not?* Also, that allowed her to offer guidance to them to deal with whatever was wrong. Obviously, if they were coming to the house to stay for an extended amount of time, something must be going wrong in their lives, right?

Right now, they were all in good places. Jillian, her youngest, was married and pregnant with her third child. She skipped law school for this life, but she seemed happy. Jonathan, the middle child, was making headway with his architectural firm and steering clear of serious romantic entanglements—as far as she knew—for now. This was good because he dealt with young, immature women anyway. And Jamison, the eldest. She finally was thriving. She was happily engaged to a fellow physician, finishing her own dermatology residency and taking a job with one of the leading dermatology clinics in the city (fingers crossed!). Her wedding was only two months away, and Margaret couldn't wait!

It was a relief to plan such a joyous occasion, given the train wrecks that had gone on in Jamie's life. For a smart girl, she was often led by her heart and not her head. But finally, Margaret could relax.

Surrounded by relative silence, with only Olivia finishing up, Margaret planned her quiet afternoon of self-care. She was going to take a quiet bubble bath, turn on her aromatherapy diffuser, and do something she hadn't had time to do in quite a while—read a book. Maybe even take a nap.

That had been worth it! In a couple of hours, the same-day movers removed all her belongings, even those that Jamie hadn't had the time to pack. They boxed everything up in an orderly fashion that would be easy for her to find in the future. This included the snack stash she kept in her closet: individually-sized packages of cookies, chips, and crackers. All shelf-stable and ready to eat in a flash. After intensive therapy, when she was a teen, she got her eating/self-esteem issues under control.

However, over the last three months, she found it was rearing its head. The desire to eat her entire stash at one time appeared in her head often. It wasn't a coincidence that wedding planning had gotten into full swing at the same time. After a session with her mother and sister, she would return to the condo and stare at the packages. It took a lot not to inhale it all. And on a practical note, she also had too much dental work to risk the vomiting that would come later. Jamie tried to reason that she didn't have an eating disorder and was merely dealing with *emotional eating.*

Either way, Jamie probably needed to visit her therapist again.

She already had a storage space from when she moved in with Eddie. So, the movers took everything there. She kept one suitcase with necessities and some clothes.

She left everything in the kitchen except her NYC mug from her modeling days. Feeling nostalgic and sad, she strolled through the condo, remembering distinct moments in different areas of the apartment—picking out furniture, watching movies with popcorn, making love in the kitchen, quizzing him about anatomy the night before a surgery. There had been a lot to love about them. If she could just stay where they were—she didn't want the next part *NOW.* If only she had told the truth earlier.

She could imagine his face when he returned to the condo—*the hurt.*

She had to do this… her eyes welled up again.

There was a small accent table by the door for keys and wallets. She unhooked the condo key from her keyring and placed it on the table. She looked down at her left hand. The diamond and sapphire ring winked at her—maybe it approved of how she was finally behaving. She slid it off, placed it on the table next to the key, and closed the door behind her, tears running down her face.

Once she got in her car, Jamie realized she didn't have a plan for the night. She could get a hotel room until she found her own place. Or she could stay with her parents. She had to think about that for a moment.

Hmmm… Probably not a good idea.

But…

She needed to tell her mother about breaking off the engagement in person before Eddie or someone else did. So, Jamie went over to her parents' home to talk to them about her decision. She could plan her next move after that.

Pulling into the circular driveway of her parents' Buckhead home. Jamie saw only one vehicle in the driveway—her mother's Black Range Rover. Her father, Gregory, rarely parked in the garage, so he wasn't home yet. Olivia's Camry was gone as well. Jamie paused, feeling trapped. She didn't want to talk to her mother about this alone; she had hoped that her father would be there to help keep the temperature down.

Should have checked before driving over here…

Give it a few minutes.

Hopefully, she had just beaten her father back to the house. No luck. She wasn't going to just sit out here for long because either her mother would see her car or a neighbor would call the police. Getting out of the Camaro, her phone rang as she walked toward the front door. Looking at the screen, she saw the call was from Eddie.

Damn! Did he already know, or was he calling to plan for their make-up discussion later tonight? Either way, she didn't want to speak to him right now. Jamie recognized she was being unfair, but she had to protect her resolve. If she heard his voice, she would crumble.

She let it go to voicemail.

Using her key, Jamie opened the front door into a quiet foyer. In fact, the entire house was quiet. It was huge, with six bedrooms, a master suite, two dining areas, and more. Jamie never understood why her parents purchased a home this large unless they expected everyone to move in one day, which would be a disaster, of course.

The study, which functioned as the family office, was to her right, and the living room and the enormous staircase, which had been a dangerous distraction during their teens, were to her left. The décor had some vintage elements and contemporary themes throughout the house: solid wood furniture with subtle neutral-colored couches and vibrant bursts of color throughout. There were several large accent rugs with both burgundy and purple; the purple was incorporated into the window treatments and the throw pillows, as well. It sounded like a lot, but it was very pretty. While she thought the house was too large, Jamie had to commend her mother's decorating skills.

She knew her mother was at home somewhere, but Jamie was creeping around as if she had no right to be in the house. Although she knew that her mother wasn't in there, her first stop was the kitchen. She knew that going into the kitchen with everything that was happening probably wasn't a good idea.

But in she went. She was right on both counts. Her mother was not there, and it wasn't a good idea. Jamie stopped and appreciated the kitchen design. The granite-topped island was huge and L-shaped, and the cabinets were a combination of maple and cherry wood. The separate bar area looked tempting, but she might have to drive, so she purposefully avoided it.

Jamie realized that, again, she hadn't eaten all day, so she peeked into the refrigerator but saw nothing she could just grab to eat. Moving to the freezer, she unearthed a half gallon of cookies and cream ice cream. *Perfect!* But the snack cabinet also yielded a greater opportunity. Margaret kept snacks—both healthy and less healthy—for her grandchildren or erstwhile children when they visited. There were several unopened boxes of Oreos that were perfect to go with the ice cream.

Pandora's Box was open for business… Jamie should have gotten a bowl to dole out a single serving, but she was all in her feelings. *Just this once…*

Jamie sat down at the kitchen island with the half-gallon container and the package of cookies. Like a kid, she crumbled the cookies directly into the 2/3s-full ice cream container. Grabbing a spoon, she dug in. At first, with each bite, she felt more soothed. After a few more, she felt more nauseous. But she didn't stop until the tub—-actually, both containers—were empty.

Ugh...she hadn't done this since she was in New York. She was a snacker by nature, but after therapy, she learned to control her feelings and her binging urges better. Her doctors diagnosed her with the eating disorder back then, and she had undergone over a year of therapy to deal with her lingering feelings about the events in NYC and her relationships with her mother and food. Seems like she should have been more proactive recently because she was falling into old patterns.

Jamie stood up from the bar and looked around furtively. This is not how she wanted Margaret to find her. There was still no sign of her mother. Maybe she was asleep.

After eating all that ice cream, she felt horrible. Jamie walked out of the kitchen and made her way up the staircase to her bedroom suite. Out of the corner of her eye, she noticed that her mother had replaced her duvet with a deep purple one. It was pretty, but she didn't stop to admire it. Making a beeline to the bathroom, she pushed up the toilet seat, grabbed her hair with one hand, and put her finger down her throat. As she threw up, she swore this was the last time.

It was amazingly quiet. A rarity. Margaret enjoyed her relaxing bubble bath, so relaxing that she almost took a nap in the porcelain tub. After getting out and drying off with one of the big white fluffy bath sheets, she decided to read a couple of magazines and one murder mystery book, at least until Gregory returned. Wrapping it around herself, Margaret padded to her bed and started applying an anti-aging lotion to her skin. She was in her mid-fifties and thought she still looked good. Her hair, which she wore in a long blunt cut, was just starting to show a significant amount of gray. Margaret had never been stick-thin like her daughter, but she had maintained her hourglass figure, even after multiple pregnancies. She worked out regularly to live as healthily as possible.

Must stay ready for the big day… she thought.

Jamison's and Eddie's wedding and reception were going to be a grand event. It was going to be held at Cha'le Gardens outside of Atlanta. With both sides wanting to invite many people, the wedding venue had to accommodate several hundred people. Getting married at a farm wasn't Jamison or Eddie's dream location, but given the situation, both reluctantly agreed. The ceremony itself would be for 200 people, but the reception would be more than double the size.

The wedding party was of moderate size. Eddie could have had a large group of men standing up for him, but he limited it to six groomsmen and one best man because Jamison had a narrower selection of women to choose from. Her daughter hadn't kept in contact with many of the models she spent time with as a teen, and her social circle in college was relatively small by choice. There had been a component of embarrassment after all that happened in NY. It took a while for her to open up to fellow students without feeling like they were looking at her with the big "P" (pregnancy) of shame on her forehead. Jamison ended up recruiting her sister, her med school roommate, one fellow dermatology resident, Eddie's sister, two former models that she did keep up with, and Felice. There was some excitement among the male members of the party that there might be more models attending the function.

Shopping for the wedding dresses was more fun than Margaret expected. Jillian was involved; however, it seemed like she enjoyed the experience more than Jamison. Jillian missed out on this part of the wedding experience because she and Richard eloped. There were going to be four outfits for the wedding day: the ceremony dress, the cocktail hour dress, the reception dress, and the going-away outfit. They already selected all four and were getting altered now. With Jamison being tall and thin, there was nothing they could buy off the rack, ready to wear.

She smiled to herself as she pulled on a velour warm-up suit. The guest list looked like a dream. *This was going to be perfect...*

Looking in the mirror, she quickly combed her hair and applied some lipstick. No one was at the house with her as far as she knew, but she was always taught to look her best—just in case. All she needed was a bottle of wine and the little tray of cheese and crackers that Olivia had left her in the fridge. Perfect for reading a book by the bay window in the master suite.

Margaret walked to the kitchen to get her snack tray and wine. But the first thing she saw was the empty ice cream container and Oreo package on the island. Two thoughts popped into her head: someone else was here, and it was probably Jamison. Her heart dropped. This scene looked like some of her daughter's negative behavior from NYC.

Margaret checked the kitchen freezer and the snack cabinet. And yes, both packages came from the house.

Oh, dear. Oh, dear. Oh, dear.

Shaken, Margaret looked in the living room and the study. *The bedroom.*

She ran up the stairs and entered Jamison's room. She could hear the retching coming from the bathroom and then crying. Margaret's heart broke. *Something must have happened...a fight with Eddie?* They hadn't fought that much as a couple, so maybe the first actual fight might have been too much to deal with.

Hopefully, it was that simple...

Jamie didn't hear her mother come into her bedroom, but she stopped short as she came out of the bathroom. *Damn...* It was obvious what had just happened: Jamie's eyes were red, and she was wiping her mouth because she had just taken a swig of mouthwash. She looked disheveled and had no time to pretty up. More evidence that it had been a bad day.

"Jamison, what happened?" Margaret asked as she walked up to her and placed an arm around her. "Come sit down. We can't let any one thing overwhelm us and force us back into old habits." They both sat down on the purple duvet-covered bed.

Jamie sighed. This is not how she wanted to have this conversation today. "Sorry, Mother. I need to get some water." She calmly said to her mother.

Without hesitation, Margaret jumped up to get a glass from the tap in the bathroom. She handed it over, and the young woman took several gulps. Jamie was thirsty. The mouthwash left a weird taste in her mouth, but she was also trying to stall.

Margaret wasn't backing down from the conversation. "I saw the ice cream and cookie containers downstairs. They were both empty. I know you are an adult now." Margaret paused. "But I'm sure you can see why this is very concerning. This is a good time in your life, but I know it's stressful. What caused this?"

Jamie inhaled deeply and wiped her eyes. She refused to look at her mother. "It's been a rough day. I've made some tough decisions that you will disagree with…"

"Did you speak with Jillian? After we left the tailor's shop, I have been questioning that reception dress…"

"No, that's not it." Jamie looked over at her mother. "What's wrong with the reception dress?" Jamie didn't like the concept of *having* a reception dress, but she thought the dress itself was gorgeous. "Never mind. It's not about the clothing for the reception or even the wedding." She steeled herself. *Here we go.* "I turned down the job with Henderson-Wu and Associates." Jamie knew she was being a chicken and leading with the least important item. But that was all she could address right then.

Margaret frowned. "Why? That job was perfect for you, your relationship, and your future children." She paused. "What did Eddie say about this? Is that what you two fought about?"

"No, that's not what we fought about. I mean, that's not all we fought about. I mean, he knows, and it surprised him…"

"Jamison, did they not offer enough flexibility? Was there something in the contract that you didn't like? You can always negotiate better terms."

"Mother, it's not that. I don't want to work there."

Margaret shook her head, confused. "OK, so where are you going to work? Are you going to take some time off after the wedding? That wouldn't be bad. You could spend some time with Eddie as a newly married couple. You could look for that house. I would not advise getting pregnant right away, though. Take some time." Margaret thought she was providing some helpful tips for married couples.

"That's not happening either, Mother."

"So, you have another job? I don't understand what's the big deal here. It's not like you two need the money." Margaret wasn't reading the room. Jamie was staring straight ahead again with her arms crossed. A little petulant, her mother thought, which made no sense.

"There is no job, Mother. There is something I need to talk to you about." *Just spit it out…* "I broke up with Eddie today."

There was silence for a few beats. Margaret felt like she had been slapped in the face. All that work to get this ungrateful child's life back in order, and she just throws it away? All the fear and anger toward Jamie destroying her life just bubbled up again.

"*How could you be so STUPID?*" Margaret said stridently.

Jamie recoiled. That was not what she expected…*but she should have*. But before she could reply, Margaret plowed on.

"You continue to make *STUPID* decisions. The job I can understand. But now, breaking up with the best thing that ever happened to you?"

Jamie tried to take the temperature down a bit. "Eddie is a good man. But I don't want to get married. I will handle canceling the venue and vendors and pay for it. I shouldn't have let the engagement get this far." She retorted in her defense.

"I don't care about the money… You are throwing away a great relationship. Over a job?" Margaret took another moment to take a couple of deep breaths. "Do you love him?"

"Yes, but I don't want to get married to him. It's not about the job—not only the job. If we got married, I would be bored and unhappy within a few years. "

"Maybe some boredom would do you some good. We know what happens when you get too much freedom."

Another dig about NY. *She would never live this down*. She let it go. "Mother, you see what just happened. I was in the bathroom throwing up after eating almost a half-gallon of ice cream and 15 Oreos. I'm not happy."

"It is cold feet. You don't exhibit enough self-control. Young people today. If it's not perfect, they want to end it. Not working through the hard times."

"What hard times? That's not what this is about." Jamie turned to her mother. "I love Eddie, I do. And if we could continue to live together and not get married—not have children at this point, if ever, I would be all for it." She pushed her hair behind her ears.

"*If ever*? Do you not want children? What is that about?"

"I don't know. Right now, the answer would be no." At the look on her mother's face, Jamie tried to take the edge off. "I don't know if I want the whole four kids and a husband right now. And that's what he wants. It's all for the best."

Margaret was reeling from all Jamie's revelations; nevertheless, she still hoped she could turn it around. But something occurred to her: she knew her daughter was not big on difficult confrontations, so she just tried to temper her comment about children. She narrowed her eyes. "So, what did Eddie say when you threw it all away?"

Jamie looked down.

"Were you woman enough to tell him to his face?" Margaret rolled her eyes. "Of course not. You knew he would convince you to stay with him. You have no backbone sometimes." Her mother looked away, then turned back with a look of resignation. "I bet you think this is all my fault, right? Like with the adoption. Yes, I am forcing you to marry and have children with this rich, handsome surgeon who loves you. I am such a horrible mother!"

Jamie felt the walls close in. Exactly why she didn't want to come to the house. Often, she found herself bending to please her mother. She hadn't been able to stand up to her mother successfully since the adoption. This felt like that: Jamie wanting to raise her baby and her mother telling her, repeatedly, how stupid an idea that was. Then Margaret contacting agencies about adoption, meetings, talking to the doctors—all like she had no voice, no agency. When she protested, her mother ignored her, and finally, she gave up. Jamie was still angry with her mother and herself about how that went down—even if it was probably the correct decision.

She also regretted her choice of father for her baby; he used drugs and died by the time she admitted she was pregnant. She didn't take care of herself because she tried to continue to work and minimize her weight gain. How did that affect her baby? Therapy had also identified all that guilt as a factor in her not wanting children now. But of course, she hadn't told Eddie about NY, so he wouldn't understand. It was just a mess.

"You need to go back and apologize. Tell him you were scared. He loves you despite the drama and mistakes from New York. How many respectable men would marry a woman who has your history?"

The words 'mistake' and 'NYC' raised Jamie's ire. "My history? What the hell does that mean? You act as if I was doing drugs and prostituting myself."

Margaret rolled her eyes and pursed her lips. "We don't know what all you were doing in NY. It wouldn't surprise me if you were dealing with unsavory men. I mean, look who you got pregnant by!" Margaret dipped her head and inhaled, then sadly looked at her daughter's face. "I shouldn't have let you go there. You obviously could not be trusted. I must take some of the responsibility for this mess."

Jamie's ears stopped working after the third sentence. "What all I was doing? What?" Jamie felt like she was falling into a deep hole. Did her mother just accuse her of being a prostitute or close to one? *What the hell…*

Jamie stood up and faced her mother. "I know I fucked up, Mother." She rarely cursed in front of her mother, but desperate times… "I know I made a huge mistake in NYC. But you *will not* let me live or live it down. I have tried and tried to make you proud of me again, respect me, hell, even like me. But I see I am wasting my time. Whenever I do anything you don't like, you tell me I make stupid decisions. After college, I went to medical school. I considered pathology, and you called it *stupid*. I wanted to do my residency on the West coast. Another *poor* decision. I wanted to cut my hair—"

"Don't you dare! Every decision you have made outside of the baby has been your own. Your unhappiness and inability to make choices that satisfy you are not my fault. I thought I raised a smarter woman than this. I take my earlier comments back. *This* is all on you."

Jamie turned to walk out.

"I am not canceling anything because you will be back after you see how ridiculous you are being. I will call Eddie and tell him you will be home soon to talk." She patted her pockets and continued yelled at Jamie's back as she descended the stairs. "My cell is downstairs. I will call when

I get it. This is why you need me as a sounding board. Left on your own, you make a mess."

Jamie heard each word and was just exhausted. She grabbed her purse from the mess on the kitchen island, where she dropped it, and walked out of the door. She was going to stay in a hotel tonight and figure out her next steps. Jamie needed some space from her mother, who essentially called her a weak-willed drug-using potential prostitute. Talking right now would not be productive and might ruin their relationship forever.

4

T Minus 6 Hours

●————————————————————●

Jamie quickly found a hotel—a LaQuinta Inn near the airport—and reserved a room using her phone.

On the way to the hotel, the young woman stopped at a nearby gas station, filled up her car, and grabbed some snacks. A bag of Cheetos and some chocolate bars were first in the basket, followed by other assorted chips and cookies. She stopped briefly in front of the alcoholic beverages. While it would have been wonderful to get drunk and sleep away the rest of this horrible, mistake-ridden day, she needed to make some plans while sober. She grabbed two large bottles of water to make herself feel healthier because she was going to inhale a lot of junk food. Eating all of this was only fair right now, because she needed some comfort. She would go back to therapy once she made it through this crisis.

Rationalization at its finest.

After checking into the hotel (with her own pillow in tow), Jamie thought she could get a little peace so she could think. She contemplated taking a bath in the small tub and started prepping a nice soak.

However, her family, ex-fiancé, and former future boss all had other ideas.

By 6:30 that night, Jamie's phone was blowing up. Eddie called every 10 minutes, and her mother alternated between those calls. Robin had even called twice. Her father slipped one call in, but his message was a reprieve from the others. He just wanted to see if she was OK.

Eddie's messages were painful to listen to—he begged her to come home. In one message, he even pledged that they wouldn't have to have kids if only she would return to him. It hurt her to hear that because it wasn't true and wasn't what he wanted. She couldn't do that to him, although it would be so easy to. There was no way out. Even if she went to the condo and told him about NYC and everything else, he would try to understand why she didn't tell him earlier—but keeping that kind of secret rots everything they built the relationship on. Really, what relationship did they have if he didn't know some of the most basic events in her life? Ones that shaped her.

But just hearing the sorrow in his voice made her rethink her choices. She hated herself and how she had treated him, which showed that she was not mature enough to be in a relationship right now. If only she had been honest with him about NYC and told him how she felt about things, they wouldn't be in this mess. They may not have dated long, but at least no one would have been hurt.

On the other hand, her mother's messages were straight infuriating. Stupid was a common word, ridiculous, regret, ungrateful… all common words on the voicemails. She could hear her father in the background admonishing Margaret about her tone and her choice of words. But that didn't change the tenor of the next round of messages.

Weary of the entire situation, Jamie got into bed. Having spent a lot of time in hotels as a model, she was leery of hotel bed covers and pillows. She tossed the bedspread and the pillows on the wooden desk in the corner. Turning on the TV, she lay under the white sheet on the bed, watching television as she screened the phone calls. She dumped pieces of the chocolate bar into the Cheetos bag and mindlessly ate the messy mixture.

After 90 minutes of almost nonstop messages, Jamie turned her phone off, but not before she fired off text messages saying she was fine and would contact them when she was ready to talk. She wasn't that familiar with GPS, but she didn't want any of the folks she was trying to avoid showing up on the hotel's doorstep. Also, while listening to these voicemails, she had another revelation: she didn't think it was possible to stay in town with all the bridges she was burning right now. However, she needed to finish her residency and get on with her life. This was a problem.

Was there a way out?

After some consideration, a plan formed that required her to turn her phone back on. Four years ago, she completed a dermatology externship as a fourth-year medical student in NY. And fortunately for her, the dermatology chief—Jennifer Raven, MD—was a fashionista and remembered her from her time on the runways. They became rather friendly, exchanging quarterly phone calls and having coffee if they saw each other at conventions or meetings. Jamie and Jennifer commiserated over being tall and the dating and shopping challenge it presented. However, the two had not had many casual conversations since Jamie's engagement, which seemed to be a pattern with her.

Had I stopped communicating with everyone once I got engaged?

However, Jennifer signed on as a reference in Jamie's job quest…*Damn it*…Did Robin reach out to Jennifer to see what was going on? More bridges burning!

But maybe Jennifer could help. Desperate times and all…

"Hello? It's Raven," a harried voice sounded on the other end. Jamie could hear Jennifer's three children, aged 10, 11, and 15, in the background, each requesting a different service or favor. Before Jamie could say anything, Jennifer said, "Hold on," and swiftly dealt with each request. Hearing the happy-sounding children in the background, Jamie wondered if she could ever be that efficient.

"Sorry! Hi, Jamie. I've been expecting you. Where are you?"

That she called Jamie by her name threw her off for a moment. "You have my number in your address book?"

"Of course. You're a friend, right?" Jennifer asked. "Let me move into another room where there's alcohol." Jennifer figured this would be a long conversation after she spoke to Robin Henderson-Wu earlier that day. She had expected a call from Jamie to explain herself. Something must be going on. The study had French doors so she could monitor her kids in the kitchen and was as good a place as any to listen to Jamie's reasoning.

At least there was alcohol available that might keep her from going off on her friend.

After pouring herself a finger (or two) of bourbon, she pushed her salt-and-pepper hair behind her ears and put her phone on speaker. "What the hell is going on with you?"

"I guess you spoke to Robin…"

"Yes. She contacted me this morning. I should be furious with you, but I figured there must be something pretty ugly going on. So, I decided to hear you out before I deleted you from my phone book." She paused. "Where are you right now? Are you safe?" Even with her stern talk, she was concerned. She knew much of Jamie's history in NY, which Jamie slowly confided to her during their friendship. Jennifer gently encouraged her to continue therapy throughout the four years of internship and residency because she felt Jamie hadn't fully dealt with her feelings and her relationship with her mother. She also suspected all of that was playing a role in the meltdown going on right now.

Jamie exhaled. "I'm safe. I'm sitting in a hotel eating Cheetos and candy bars."

"Nutritious. What happened? Stop stalling."

"I set my world on fire today. May the bridges I burn light the way."

Silence as Jennifer took a sip of her drink.

I need her help. She's not going to make it easy for me, Jamie thought. The flood gates opened…words tumbled out. "I ended my engagement, turned down the job offer, and I am binging again and hiding from my mother, Eddie, and Robin. Right now, I hate everything. I have made such a gigantic mess of my life." She was crying silently, but Jennifer could hear the muffled sniffling.

"OK. OK. I'm sorry you blew your life up. I will get the details after you work them out in therapy. What do you think I can do?"

"I need to get out of town. I just need a one-month dermatology rotation anywhere—all my mandatory stuff is done. They don't have to pay me…"

"You sound like a fugitive. Are you sure you want to run away like this? Are you sure you and your fiancé can't work this out?"

"We *could* work it out. That's the problem. It would require someone to sacrifice things that are important to them. We would hate each other," Jamie exhaled wearily. "It's all my fault. I let things slide. Just went along to get along. Didn't say no to things I knew I didn't want."

"Why would you do that? This is your life."

"I was trying to be someone I thought he would want as opposed to who I am. It's complicated."

"So that means it's about your mother." Jennifer grew quiet.

"So, can you help me? I can't stay here, because I'm setting up a real whodunit here with me as the victim. I need to clear my head and escape before there is a Dateline episode about me."

"Well, you had me at no pay. I need to verify all this with your program chief…"

"Who hates me now…I've embarrassed the program by turning down the job like this."

"That means the dermatology chief will be glad to see you go. Man, you truly torched everyone, huh? What are you going to do after you finish?

"I need to make a fresh start and figure out what I want." Jamie chuckled through the tears. "I also need some therapy."

Jennifer laughed briefly. "Don't we all? We need a plausible reason that you need to leave." There were a few moments of silence as they both considered this. Then Jennifer spoke. "I have an idea. Have you heard of Doctors Overseas?"

Jamie took a swig of water. "Vaguely," she replied.

"You go work in horribly underserved areas in other countries: war-torn, famine, or drought-stricken. I think it might give you some perspective. You will be away from the situation and can clear your head. Get some distance… And it's a suitable cover for why you are finishing up elsewhere."

Jennifer was thinking on the fly. "But, damn! You don't have enough experience post-residency, but you are fluent in—is it French and Spanish? I can put in a good word. I know one of the CEOs. We should be able to find a way around it."

That sounded like an intriguing option. No one she was trying to avoid could pop in on her without an invitation… *sign me up.* "How long would I have to stay? Not like I want to come back here any time soon."

"For all the rules we will bend to get you there, for at least a year? Are you willing to do that? How about this? You fly up this weekend. Monday, I will set you up with an interview with Doctors Overseas and get you out of your current program if they haven't booted you out already. Tuesday or Wednesday, you can cover this clinic out in the wilderness. Not really in the wilderness, but it's in a rural area. No one wants to go there because there is not much to do. We have to keep the clinic open because of some legal mumbo jumbo, so you can finish up there. After you finish, off to Africa you go." Jennifer was excited about this solution and planned to pour herself another finger of bourbon to congratulate herself.

Whew! Jamie didn't even take long to decide how she felt about this. *People without many options…*

"Thank you! I will be on the first flight I can get out of here this weekend." Jamie stopped. "Why are you helping me? You're standing on one bridge I'm burning," she asked.

"If this had been solely about your mother, I might have let you twist in the wind. You should have dealt with that shit already, and hopefully, you will now, since you see how it fucks you up." Jennifer finished her bourbon. "But I know how it is to bend yourself into a pretzel for your relationship and not know who you are and how to get out. At least you didn't have kids—you figured that part out before that happened."

Jamie agreed. Bringing a child into her current dysfunction would have been horrifying.

Jennifer continued. "You can even crash with my kids and me for a couple of days until you get yourself situated. I plan to go to a couple of spas while you are here and not have to spring for a sitter," Jennifer joked. "You'll need to reserve a room at this specific hotel in the area—at least during the week when you are covering the wilderness clinic. But get ready. I think you'll have a babysitting job every weekend."

"I appreciate that. I appreciate all of this. Jennifer, I am so sorry to have gotten you involved in this mess." Jamie stopped again. "Aren't your kids teenagers? Who am I babysitting?"

"Only one is a teenager, and that's why you're watching all of them. They are mischief makers! But otherwise, you'll be doing me a favor. I don't have to wrestle residents for one month to get them to cover that office." Jennifer walked out of the study to check on her kids, carrying her phone. "I'm glad we found a solution to your problem. But man, for such a normal-seeming person, you are the most chaotic person I have ever met."

I'm sorry?

It's not like Jamie hadn't heard that comment before. She thanked her friend for saving her ass again and rang off.

95

5
Time

It was a rough night. Questions about every move she made over the past 48 hours kept dancing around in her head—really major doubts.

She could go back...

A little voice kept repeating it, but her common sense kept reciting all the reasons her current course of action was for the best. She had burned those bridges.

All that chatter in her head kept her from sleeping. After she finished the Cheetos and chocolate concoction, she longed for alcohol and hit the minibar. Unfortunately, rum and coke didn't help her sleeplessness at all. By the morning, Jamie was wrung out but resolute. Also, she couldn't change now. She paid a pretty penny for a last-minute flight to NYC. She hated throwing away good money.

Because the flight was scheduled for midafternoon, she had all morning to finish her last-minute errands. Maybe she could get a little nap in because she had tossed and turned all night. Jamie had turned her phone back on when she made her plane reservation and left it on vibrate. Fortunately, the "leave me alone" text messages had stopped the incoming call barrage for the night.

However, Jon called her first thing on Saturday morning with the sun just peeking over the horizon. "Why aren't you answering your phone?" he barked at her once she picked up. The annoyance was obvious.

It was too early to get out of bed, but she needed to talk to him.

"I didn't want to talk to anyone last night. But it seems no one would get the hint." She grabbed the remote for the TV and turned it on. Besides, I sent texts telling everyone I was fine. You weren't calling me last night, anyway. Who told you?"

"You know I got calls from Mother and Eddie. They both thought I was hiding you from the consequences of your actions." He paused, then continued. "So, I got an earful. While I was on a date, mind you."

"Sorry. Maybe Peyton will see the folly of her relationship with you. The Scott family is a dating nightmare. She can get out while the getting's good." Jamie checked her watch and sat up in bed. "I need to get my stuff together…"

She paused when she realized Jon did not know what she was talking about. "I'm sorry. You are the first to know. I'm leaving town. Everything is such a disaster. I need some space."

Jon sighed. "I figured as much. You pissed everyone off at the same time. It's nice not to be the black sheep of the family right now!" he chuckled quietly and then sobered up. "What about your residency? You are so close to being finished. And where are you going?"

She quickly explained her Hail Mary plan. Jon chuckled again. "Leave it to you to step—no lay in—a pile of crap and still come out smelling like a rose."

"We'll see how this will go. I'm not resting on my laurels yet."

"Are you calling Mother, Dad? Jillian? Eddie? Let them know what you're doing," he asked.

"Before I get to NY? No. That's why you know the details, so they won't think I died." *Maybe they might want to kill her themselves...* "I'm willing to cancel all the venues and reservations for the wedding, but I think I will leave a checkbook with you for you to give Mother the money for cancellation fees."

"Not the right move, I think. But you have to do you."

"Dad's the only one besides you I wasn't fighting with yesterday. I think cooler heads need to prevail before someone says something ugly that we can't take back. I mean, Mother danced pretty close to that line yesterday and might have stuck a toe over it." Jamie quickly relayed the last conversation with their mother, to Jon's embarrassment.

"I will reach out after a while—just to let things blow over." Carrying her cell phone, she headed to the bathroom to splash some water on her face. "Oh, yeah! I want you to keep the Camaro. Keep it registered and drive it around a little. I will bring it to your house and get an Uber to the airport."

"Nooooo! Must I keep that gas-guzzling loud old-ass car? What do I get out of it?" Jon protested.

"My eternal gratitude. And the chance to impress girls with a genuine muscle car!" Jamie teased.

Jon mumbled with fake indignation, but quickly relented. "I'm going to miss you, Jamie-Jay. Please keep in touch while you are away. I was happy that you were planning to live here for good."

"I mean. I will be gone for what? One year? You won't even know I'm gone…"

✳✳✳

After leaving her car at Jon's home around noon, Jamie caught an Uber to the airport. Her phone rang halfway through her trip. Thinking it was Jon calling to complain about the car, she didn't check the display and answered.

It was Margaret.

"Hello, Jamison."

Damn… "Good afternoon, Mother."

"Jamison, where are you? I heard from Jon. Something about you leaving town? Where are you going?"

Jon and his big mouth. "I'm finishing my residency up north, and then I'm leaving the country. I am going to Africa for a few months to work and get my head together."

"So, you're calling the wedding off? I thought this was temporary. I can't believe this…"

"It's for the best. I will pay the cancellation fees and call the vendors if you need me to. Jon has my checkbook." Jamie swallowed and allowed the feelings of sorrow and regret to wash over her. While she sounded composed, she was truly upset about the drastic changes in her life. She had expected one future, and now her future was unknown by her own doing, too. Most of her relationships were in flux, including the one with her mother. While that relationship could be challenging at the best of times, right now, it was a flaming dumpster fire. "I am sorry, Mother. I'm being horrible right now, but I have to get out."

"Have you talked to Eddie?"

"I can't talk to him right now. I need him to hate me so he can move on."

"I really don't know what to say to you right now. You are going to regret this decision. All these decisions made in haste…"

Before her mother could call her ungrateful or stupid, Jamie cut her off. "Maybe I will, Mother. But I have to get myself sorted out. I'm sorry—I have made an insane number of mistakes over the past couple of years. I'll try to contact Eddie after a bit, but not now. You and I can talk later. I think we both need to cool down."

"I hope you find what you are looking for. I'm not sure how I feel about what you are doing." Margaret hung up.

She didn't either… but it would only be for a year. Then things could get back to normal.

D. W. Brooks

Author, Physician, Kidney Transplant Survivor

I have always been an enthusiastic reader. Breakfast in my childhood home was a slow process as I would read any object on the table—newspapers, cereal boxes, milk cartons, anything. Taking away my books was an effective punishment.

As part of this interest, my cousins and I created a neighborhood of preteen and teenage characters who had adventures and solved mysteries. We drew out this neighborhood, identified where everyone lived, and created character profiles for each one. We were well ahead of our time and wrote a lot of unfinished stories which disappeared into the attic as we got older. After this failed experiment, I still had thoughts of writing my own stories one day.

Becoming an author was an early dream pushed aside by practical thoughts and fears. I decided to take a more surefire route of going to medical school and residency. While I didn't write my own stories, I spent time writing in a medical and education capacity.

A health crisis awakened the desire to write again. And the ability to self-publish, I could see a path to getting my words and stories out of my head and into a bound book others can read and hopefully enjoy.

The author lives in Texas with her husband and children. She enjoys trying to stay in shape, sporadically cooking, reading (still), writing, and working on her blog. She is eternally grateful to the woman who donated a kidney to her over 5 years ago and continues to advocate for organ donation as much as she can.

To learn more about D. W. Brooks and future publications and events, visit https://authordwbrooks.com.

9 7 9 8 9 8 9 0 8 0 7 3 1